the Enchanted Attic

BOOK TWO

Saving Moby Dick

L.L. SAMSON

ZONDER**kidz**

ZONDERVAN.com/
AUTHOR**TRACKER**
follow your favorite authors

ZONDERKIDZ

Saving Moby Dick
Copyright © 2012 by L. L. Samson

This title is also available as a Zondervan ebook.
Visit www.zondervan.com/ebooks

Requests for information should be addressed to:
Zonderkidz, 5300 Patterson Ave., S.E., Grand Rapids, Michigan 49530

Library of Congress Cataloging-in-Publication Data

Samson, L. L., 1964-
    Saving Moby Dick / L.L. Samson.
        p. cm. – (Enchanted attic series ; bk. 2)
        Summary: Orphaned fourteen-year-old twins Linus and Ophelia and their
    friend Walter think they can control the powers of the enchanted attic, but their
    plans backfire when they bring crazy Captain Ahab from the book world into the
    real world.
        ISBN 978-0-310-72797-2 (softcover)
        [1. Space and time—Fiction. 2. Characters in literature—Fiction. 3. Melville,
    Herman, 1819-1891. Moby Dick—Fiction. 4. Books and reading—Fiction. 5. Brothers
    and sisters—Fiction. 6. Twins—Fiction. 7. Orphans—Fiction.] I. Title.
    PZ7.S1696Sav 2012
    [Fic–dc23   2012020164

All Scripture quotations, unless otherwise indicated, are taken from the Holy Bible, *New
International Version®, NIV®*. Copyright © 1973, 1978, 1984, 2011 by Biblica, Inc.™ Used by
permission. All rights reserved worldwide.

Any Internet addresses (websites, blogs, etc.) and telephone numbers in this book are
offered as a resource. They are not intended in any way to be or imply an endorsement
by Zondervan, nor does Zondervan vouch for the content of these sites and numbers
for the life of this book.

Zonderkidz is a trademark of Zondervan.

Cover design: Kris Nelson
Interior design: Ben Fetterley

Printed in the United States of America

---

12 13 14 15 16 17 /DCI/ 26 25 24 23 22 21 20 19 18 17 16 15 14 13 12 11 10 9 8 7 6 5 4 3 2 1

Saving Moby Dick

Contents

one

Getting Caught Up with a Cougar on Your Tail

Or Layering in a Bit of Backstory While Running Your Pants off in the Present

Don't let those young people tell you I didn't warn them, because I most certainly did! In fact, I was one of the first people to hear about the cougar that somehow made its way to the town of Kingscross, New York, which is where I live and work and buy my books from Seven Hills Better Books on Rickshaw Street. And that bookstore is where I first met fourteen-year-old twins, Linus and Ophelia Easterday, and their aunt and uncle—who happen to own the bookshop— Portia and Augustus Sandwich (also twins). I've been a regular fixture (customer) there ever since.

How the cougar incident actually happened, I don't know. I suppose I could make up something posthaste (right away), but how that cougar arrived is clearly not the point of this story. Stories like that are reserved for syrupy motion pictures about animal journeys, like *The Incredible Journey* or nature channel documentaries, which are a bit more believable.

By the same token, this story is not necessarily believable. It may be even more unbelievable than the idea of a cat, a dog, and a guinea pig making their way across the Cascades (a mountain range that runs through Washington, Oregon, and the eastern edge of Northern California).

Rather, this story is about our three friends (the Easterday twins and Walter) and what happened when they encountered a crazy man named Captain Ahab—although if you asked the captain, he'd probably say the cougar is precisely the point of this story. What Captain Ahab means is that the cougar provided an epiphany (a time of great enlightenment, an "A-Ha" moment) for him. But more on that later. Let's not get too far ahead of ourselves before even three hundred words have been set down on paper, for then I wouldn't have created the suspense one needs to keep turning pages.

This story begins on a hot day in July. Walter, Linus, and Ophelia were walking down a path along the Bard River and skipping stones—or whatever it is young people do these days—when the cougar made its presence known.

You may recall that Linus and Ophelia were recently orphaned by their parents—Drs. Ron and Antonia Easterday, two lepidopterologists (scientists who specialize in the collection and study of butterflies and moths) who are studying never-before-seen specimens on the South Pacific island of Willis; so the twins now live in Kingscross with their Aunt Portia and Uncle Augustus. (What you just read is known as a run-on sentence. Clearly I could have made all of those words fit into at least two sentences, if not three. Some writers of the more spare school of style would have cut the word count in half. And I say, "Good for them!" I, however, write like I talk. It keeps the tone conversational, which is what I'm aiming for.)

Now back to the Bard River. The cougar jumped down from a tree and right onto the path in front of the three young teenagers. Everyone froze—Linus, Ophelia, and their good friend Walter. He lives next door to the bookshop at The Pierce School for Young People, a would-be snooty preparatory school run by Ms. Madrigal Pierce. *(Strictly off the record, she's a real looker.)* The three of them had become inseparable friends just a month before when they first discovered the enchanted circle in the twins' attic. *(And oh, was that an adventure!)*

The cougar, which was about the size of a Labrador retriever—but much more dangerous and not nearly as annoying—froze as well. But the big cat kept his face as deadpan (expressionless) as Linus. *(The boy rarely lets on what he's thinking. You just have to assume he's listening to you.)* The fur on the cougar's tawny coat stood up at the back of his neck.

"What do we do?" whispered Walter. This athletic, good-looking British boy, who could pick a lock in two seconds or less, was ready to bolt. He was figuring, quite mistakenly, that he had a chance of outrunning the beast.

"Don't move," whispered Ophelia. To the casual observer, this petite, brown-eyed girl seemed quite calm, cool, and collected. But Linus knew better. Even out of the corner of his eye, he could tell his sister was trembling all over—even her headful of dark curls were quivering with nervous energy. (And since the top of Ophelia's head came only to the middle of Linus's chest, he had a perfect bird's-eye view.)

Looking to be her exact opposite in every way, Linus is Ophelia's lanky, six-foot-tall twin brother with stick-straight blond hair and bright blue eyes. They looked about as alike as the president of the United States and the Queen of England. (The pair does have similar toes, however.)

As Linus now stared back at—or should I say, *stared down upon*—the big cat, he attempted to communicate with the animal telepathically (brain to brain). At age fourteen Linus was a lad of few words, and he was always trying to find ways to speak even fewer.

The cat stepped toward them.

Easy does it, Linus thought, trying to focus his thoughts right at the beast's forehead. *We taste terrible. Seriously.*

The cat took another step.

Really, cat. Walter tastes like gym socks left in the corner of a locker for six months. Ophelia tastes like old novels someone pulled out of a dead aunt's sweater drawer—including the mothballs. And as for me, I taste like thrift store clothing, tattered tennis shoes, and Hi Karate aftershave. (He'd found an old bottle in the medicine cabinet that morning and had unfortunately dabbed some on.)

The cougar's eyes widened, and he growled low in his throat. He then pawed a small pile of old leaves, took a pee, turned and loped (ran with bounding steps) down the path. The cougar was simply marking his territory. Male cougars are solitary creatures. Do not mess with their boundaries because they're much better than most people at protecting them.

Was it Linus' powers of mental telepathy that diverted the little group from a situation of carnage and mayhem (slaughter and violence)? Possibly. *(Or perhaps the cougar was simply full from having just eaten several rabbits out of a hutch behind the house of the professor of sustainable urban agriculture at nearby Kingscross University.)*

Walter blew out a sigh and ran a hand through his wavy brown hair. "I'm not sure what just happened, but whatever it was, it was brilliant!" His green-blue eyes were gleaming with the excitement of the wildlife encounter.

Ophelia threw herself onto the nearest park bench and pushed her hair off her face. She held out a hand for the boys to see. "Look how much I'm shaking."

Linus shoved his hands in his pockets and looked around. They needed to get home. Uncle Augustus was throwing another theme party the next night *and* he'd told the twins in no uncertain terms that they needed to be in his costume collection room at 5 P.M. sharp to pick out their outfits and then help with the final arrangements. Linus and Ophelia had roped poor Walter into serving hors d'oeuvres with them, believing fully in the old adage that misery loves company. In other words, if you have something you'd rather not do, you might as well bring your best friend along and let him suffer as well.

As I mentioned earlier, Seven Hills Better Books, run by Portia Sandwich, plied its wares (sold its stuff) on Rickshaw Street. Last month, most of its merchandise was destroyed by a flash flood. But even before the dam on the Bard River burst and the shop flooded, there had never been a new book in the place. So the shop smelled even mustier now, a bit like old paper, leather, mildew, and coffee, which Portia drank from dawn to dusk. (From dawn to dusk *is what's known as a cliché. An overused expression. Used occasionally, however, it can make a reader feel at home in the pages of the book. But the writer must feel fine about sacrificing a little respect for the good of the reader. Nobody tells you that in college!)*

The two sets of twins lived on the two floors above the bookshop. *(It's actually three floors, if you count the attic— and oh my friends, you simply must count the attic!)* Linus and Ophelia mostly kept the place clean.

You might as well go ahead and feel sorry for them. Deserted by their parents *(who don't deserve to have such fine children, the louts!)* for some island in the South Pacific, and then having to live with two eccentric, never-married relatives *(who really are delightful, they're just clueless about children)*, Linus and Ophelia were so bored most of the time, they actually didn't mind doing their chores. Ophelia jumped out of bed early each morning to cook breakfast, while Linus swept the sidewalk in front of the bookshop.

All right! All right! That's all a lie. I was simply trying to help your parents by making Linus and Ophelia appear to be model teenage citizens. They hate doing their chores as much as you hate doing yours. And sometimes they have to be asked multiple times to do them. At least that was true when they still lived with their parents. Uncle Augustus runs a tighter ship. (He asks only once. I'll let you draw your own conclusions as to why that works for him.)

Linus, Ophelia, and Walter made their way down the main aisle of the shop. The damaged books had been carted away, and all the mud that the river had deposited inside the store last month had been mopped up long ago. Despite that, a smell remained—an odor of old river grass and mud and what you might imagine a snail smells like if you were to press your nose against its shell and take a deep breath. *(Oh dear! Perfectly horrid.)*

"Hello, Aunt Portia!" Ophelia said as they walked past the office. The older woman was wearing a bright orange mu-mu (a flowing sort of tent dress that was fashionable in the 1960s), and her frizzy, apricot-colored hair was mostly hidden under a yellow headscarf. She was checking her inventory of books against remaining stock.

"Ophelia, darling. Grab me another stack, would you?"

Linus spun around and grabbed a tower of leather-bound volumes for Portia. He felt sorry for his aunt. Nobody as generous and creative as Aunt Portia should have to lose half her business.

"Thanks, lovey. Headed to the costume room?"

Linus nodded. "I get to be one of the harpooneers."

"Not fair!" cried Walter. "He gets one of the good parts, and I'm Pip the cabin boy—the *incoherent* cabin boy, I might add. At least Uncle Auggie *says* he's incoherent."

"He's right," said Ophelia. *(She's the literature reader of the Twins Easterday.)*

"And you?" Portia pointed at Ophelia.

"Well, seeing as there are basically no women to speak of in *Moby-Dick*, I get to be the innkeeper's wife near the beginning of the book."

"The one that makes all that chowder?" asked Portia.

"Yep."

"How exciting!" She clapped. "A Whale of a Tale Seafood Fest. Auggie outdid himself this time. And we're serving chowder, too!"

How not exciting, thought Linus. *Speaking of chowder ...*

"Speaking of chowder," said Ophelia, "what's for dinner?"

Walter involuntarily winced. Portia's meals were a tad bizarre. They were usually themed to a certain ingredient or a particular color—sometimes both.

"It's yellow day."

Corn. Summer squash. Yukon Gold potatoes. Macaroni and cheese. Linus couldn't think of any other yellow foods, and Aunt Portia didn't offer any further details beyond the color. But he didn't mind. That boy will eat whatever is around. Ophelia, on the other hand, is such a picky eater that she'd be nothing but a walking skeleton if she didn't make herself PB&Js at least twice a day.

"All right," Ophelia said as she headed up the stairs to the residence. "See you at seven."

"Want to eat with us, Walt?" asked Linus.

"I think I'll take my chances at Madrigal's tonight," he said, shoving his hands in the pockets of his khaki (dull yellowish brown) shorts. *(Ophelia once confided in me how much she loves Walter's British accent, although she'd rather shave her head than let anyone else know this little detail.)*

"Suit yourself," said Ophelia, thinking she'd be sure to save him a plate. Walter had a whale of an appetite. It had to be due to all the push-ups he did throughout the day.

Uncle Augustus was waiting for them with three outfits arranged on an antique red velvet sofa that, quite honestly, deserved to support only empty clothes, due to its extreme lack of comfort. *(If you ever want your guests to stay for only fifteen minutes or less, buy yourself one of those awful things.)*

Ophelia grabbed her long skirt, blouse, and apron, as well as a white mobcap (the hat that Little Miss Muffet wears) and headed off to her bedroom to change. The boys stayed in the costume room. Linus donned breeches (knee-length pants), a vest, and some feathered leather ties that made him look like—or tried to, anyway—an island native trying to dress like a whaleman. Considering Linus's fair skin and light blond hair, it was about as effective a look as an electric car trying to keep pace on the Autobahn (a high-speed expressway in Germany). Walter, wearing knickers (loose-fitting short pants gathered at the knee) and a voluminous homespun (too big and very plain) shirt, just looked a mess.

"Perfect!" cried Augustus, clapping his slender hands together. One look at him and you knew what Linus would look like when he was in his seventies. While Linus and Ophelia display almost no physical similarities (other than their toes), Portia and Augustus resemble one another the way a salt shaker resembles a pepper shaker, excepting for the obvious detail of gender. They both stand tall and straight while holding their slim rib cages aloft. And they both possess that soft, dripping candle wax variety of skin that vibrates a bit when they talk. Which is often. They're quite the chatty, social pair.

Ophelia returned, her dark curls shining against the white of her blouse. When Walter's eyes widened at the sight of her, she blushed and quickly turned to her uncle. "Well?"

"Lovely, my dear. All right, then. You three are to report, in costume, at six o'clock tomorrow evening—and be ready to receive your orders from Ronda."

Ronda lives on the other side of Seven Hills, runs her own hair salon, and does catering on the side. Everyone loves Ronda. *(She's a real looker too, and that's not necessarily off the record.)*

"Aye, aye, Cap'n." Walter saluted.

Linus wondered if there was time for a quick PB&J before dinner.

"I'm having a sandwich after I get out of this thing," said Ophelia. "Anybody else want one?"

Both boys did. After all, Ophelia wasn't stingy with the peanut butter or the jelly. And the jelly was always home-made. And let's be realistic. They had to fortify themselves in anticipation for that yellow meal which might well have been yellow squash five different ways.

two

Considering the Visit of a Madman
Or Let's Bring on a Sense of Anticipation for the Reader

The trio sat on a blue velvet couch with gold fringe that the previous owner of the three-story town house, Cato Grubbs, had left behind. He'd pretty much deserted the place the twins had come to assume. Portia and Augustus then bought the building for such a low price, they almost felt guilty. But they needed a place right away. Their old building, much the same arrangement, had caught fire up on the third floor (though no one was ever up there). However, the very next day they'd found a flyer in their mailbox (from some real estate agent who'd most likely been canvasing the neighborhood) extolling (praising) the glories of the green stone building (think Statue of Liberty green) on Rickshaw Street. Sold!

The three teens now stared at the white circle painted on the wooden floor of the secret attic—a magical place that the twins had accidentally discovered the month before.

"It's July tenth."

"That makes tomorrow the eleventh," said Walter.

Don't judge Walter too harshly for that statement of the obvious. He has his reasons.

Ophelia patted her copy of *Moby-Dick* that she'd been

reading in preparation for the next night's "Whale of a Tale" dinner party. "Do you really think after Quasimodo that we want to risk bringing another character across from Book World?"

"Quasi was a great guy," said Walter.

Linus nodded.

"I really miss him." Ophelia crossed her legs beneath her.

"I'd hate to think we wouldn't take advantage of this again." Walter dropped to the floor and began doing push-ups, his brown, curly hair (just a touch too long) flopping about as he raised and lowered his body to the floor with practiced ease. He always tried to stay in good shape.

"Me too," said Linus.

"Father Lou warned us." Ophelia let her doubt show. The trio had come to respect the hippie priest from the parish across the street who proved himself dependable and trustworthy last time the enchanted circle opened up and the hunchback of Notre Dame came through. "But, imagine ..."

The adventure they'd shared—thanks to mad scientist Cato Grubbs's enchanted circle—still electrified them. Cato had discovered how to bring fictional *(for all you dullards, that means made up in the imagination of the author)* characters to life in the here and now. And the friendship they'd formed with the hunchback of Notre Dame, Quasimodo himself, would never really die. Sometimes it seemed as if a vital part of their group had gone missing. Perhaps that was the case.

"At any rate," said Ophelia, "the only really interesting character in *Moby-Dick* is Captain Ahab, and he's going to be a handful compared to Quasi."

The next evening, at 11:11 P.M., the portal would open. It did so only once a month.

"Summertime is the time to do this." Walter stood and wiped the sweat from his forehead with the hem of his T-shirt. "I can't imagine telling characters to sit tight until we get out of class."

"But have you read *Moby-Dick*?" Ophelia asked. "Captain Ahab is full-blown insane, and as I understand it, his mental illness only gets worse. Maybe Father Lou is right."

"Maybe," said Linus.

Walter began retying his sneakers. "There's another question, too. Do you have time to finish reading that book in three days?"

"I'll read all night tonight and that should give me plenty of time to finish."

Linus nodded. His sister could read *fast*. She sure did it often enough. As for him, he preferred *doing* things: building model planes, making small machines, experimenting with the lab equipment that Cato Grubbs had left behind. *That* had become a most interesting past time and one he kept to himself. Sometimes a young man has to have secrets.

The group disassembled for the night; but later that evening, Linus crept back up the stairs, ready to continue what Cato Grubbs had begun. Or in all actuality, he hoped to catch up to Cato. You see, he knew Cato could now bring characters forth wherever and whenever he chose. What Linus didn't know was how long they could stay when Cato brought them over in Cato's newfound way. Of course, Linus would love to discover how it all worked to begin with, but that would take time, lots and lots of time.

When Quasimodo unexpectedly emerged from the circle

last month, and they found Cato's old instruction book, the teens knew they had only sixty hours before the portal opened up again, sixty hours to hide a medieval bell ringer, sixty hours until—if he didn't make it back into the circle in time—Quasi would implode and hiss and smoke, much like the Wicked Witch of the West in *The Wizard of Oz*.

Does this make me a mad scientist in training? Linus asked himself, hoping the answer to the question was yes.

Ophelia knew exactly where Linus was headed when he snuck past her room and headed toward Uncle Auggie's costume room. You see, the door to the secret attic was behind a set of red velvet curtains that pretended to shade a window (only to those people who were idiotic enough not to realize there could be no window on an inside wall). But those who pushed the drapery aside to investigate wouldn't see anything special. The door to the attic seemed to be only a wall of crumbling plaster, and the wooden lath was clearly visible where chunks of plaster had once been.

Ophelia pictured Linus pressing on the lower right corner and releasing the spring—which is exactly what Linus was doing.

Now, you must remember that Linus and Ophelia are twins, which means they have more of a chance of having some odd connection between them than you and I would have. Oh heavens! Especially if you haven't had a bath today—then I wouldn't want you anywhere near me. Thanks to my important work at the University, I always have cleaning products handy. So you might want to make sure you're not close enough for me to spray a nice strong bleach solution your way. I've been known to do that in the past and I wouldn't hesitate to do it again.

Linus stepped quietly up the narrow staircase, bending his head to enter the room at the top. Linus's head barely skimmed that part of the ceiling where the two slopes meet in the middle. He lit a candle on the lab table where all of Cato Grubbs's equipment once sat gathering dust, but now ...

He lit another candle on the desk.

The lab would have made anyone look around with awe. I know it affected me the same way the first time I entered the dim and musty space that smells like old shoes, horse-hair, hot dogs, and geraniums. Lining the front and back walls are shelves that hold vials and bottles and baskets all neatly arranged and labeled. Ginger. Cardamom. Pekoe. Mr. Grubbs's very stale tea stash. I suppose every mad scientist has his or her beverage of choice And picturing him sitting there with his books while sipping on a mug of tea makes perfect sense. Linus's is Alpine Dew, an insufferable soda holding promises of caffeine overload and rotting teeth.

The baskets held odd bits of junk, most of it very old and seemingly workaday. Nuts, bolts, hinges, nails, bits of fabric, leather, popsicle sticks, and silver cutlery (knife, spoon, fork). Clear glass bottles of varying sizes displayed liquids that seemed to glow from the single ray of candlelight. They shone in a variety of colors—sometimes from within the same bot-tle! Three jars of powder labeled ONE, TWO, and THREE sat next to a mortar and pestle on a shelf above the worktable. The requisite (necessary) scientific apparatus (equipment)—complete with tubes and beakers and burners—rested under a layer of dust on a table near the door.

On Cato's desk, an old library table with the finish scraped off in most places, sat stacks of colorful books with names like *Bringing the Imaginary to Life: A Proposition*.

Or *Trapdoors to Other Realms*. And of course there were the old standbys, like *Simple Chemistry to Wow Your Simple Friends (They'll Think You're a Magician!)* and *Stage Presence—Stage Presents: The Art of Showing Up and Showing Off*. It seems even old Cato was looking for an angle to make a little money. Classics like *The History of Alchemy, Physics for Nincompoops*, and *Mixing it Up with Common Chemicals* were also there, as well as many more older and smellier books—dare I say, mildew strewn—that were written in German. Others used an alphabet that no one recognizes today. Perhaps you would—although I dearly hope not. These books were the most threadbare and the most obscure (unknown by most people), and they were also the most apt to send chills down your spine. It's best to leave them alone.

So you can see that Linus had a lot to work with. In some ways he thought bringing forth literary characters at will—not just on the eleventh of the month—would be quite the accomplishment. But what if, more importantly, he happened upon the formula for an inexpensive-to-produce airplane fuel? Now *that* would be worth something!

He pulled down powder number three, pushed off the cork stopper with his thumbs, and set to work.

three

A Whale of a Party

Or Introducing the Neighbors and Other Characters That Play Minor Roles

Even though I was invited to this Moby Dick themed party (the first time I'd ever received one of Augustus Sandwich's coveted invitations), you won't ingest (take into you) this chapter from my perspective. I'm the narrator, Bartholomew Inkster, self-taught literary fussbudget. This means I'm telling the story. And how did I come by all this information, you might ask? Good question, my dears! You see, the twins and Walter told me about it themselves when they became students at Kingscross University. My little office became the place for many a story and many cups of peppermint tea, and not one of them left my office with any sort of dirt on their shoes, I can tell you that!

Heavens, but I lost my focus there for a moment. I wanted to tell you about limited point of view. Limited point of view feels complicated when explained by dullards and dunces, but it's simply this: Pick a character you want to walk around as. You might even picture yourself in a control room inside that person's brain, as if he or she is a robot you're control-ling. The character's eyes are your windows. And then you write only what that person can see, feel, hear, taste, touch, and think. What anybody else is thinking is left to your character's best guess.

So in this chapter, I'll only relay what's in Walter's head and what Walter's senses tell him. I'm choosing Walter due to the fact that he's going to get a crush on someone, and we'd most likely enjoy his reactions.

Oh, and you should also know that most of this book is written in the omniscient (all-knowing) point of view. In other words, we can listen in on everyone's thoughts. This makes sense since I interviewed everyone involved and took, dare I say it, comprehensive and cogent (lots of clear) notes— notes over which my colleagues in the English department at Kingscross University would feel envious. (They truly don't appreciate me there, the louts!)

Ahem.

Sometimes caterer, sometimes cosmetologist, Ronda tapped Walter on the arm. And like most red-blooded males, he became a bundle of fumbles (clumsy) around her. Ronda is that pretty. That evening she'd pulled her mahogany hair back into a fashionable ponytail, and she wore all black— which made her aquamarine eyes sparkle all the more. I daresay Ronda could have been pulled from the pages of *Vogue* magazine.

"Now, Walter, honey. Take this little plate here to Professor Birdwistell. He's recently become vegan (a person who eats nothing that comes from animals), and I told him I'd make something special for him." She winked.

Walter nearly dropped the plate of crudité. *(It's pronounced crew-dih-tay, and it's really nothing more than a fancy name for raw vegetables, which is always the most disappointing offering on any buffet, if you ask me.)* Next to the vegetables on the tray was a little dish of dipping sauce, which Walter couldn't name. But the aroma reminded him of teriyaki. Walter ate a lot of takeaway food back in his home-town of London, England, thanks to his mother's long hours at work.

As Walter walked down the steps and into the bookshop, Mr. Birdwistell (pronounced "bird whistle")—a puffed-up, pompous bag of wind who's a ridiculously self-important *(calm down, Bartholomew!)* professor in the Philosophy department at Kingscross University—took the plate without even a thank-you. As for his physical description? Picture a plump, mean old bird wearing an old suit. That's Birdwistell for you. I thank the good Lord everyday I don't have to clean up after that man.

Walter shrugged. Unlike American children, he didn't expect adults to notice him and fawn all over him. And besides, he could head back up to the kitchen to receive more instructions from Ronda, a much more pleasing proposition.

She enlisted his help in cutting up a block of cheddar and chatted with him while he worked. Walter concentrated on the knife. Even the sound of her voice made him lose focus.

"So how do you like it over at The Pierce School, Walter?"

"All right—since classes haven't started yet. There are just two students living there now: myself and Clarice Yardly-Poutsmouth. She eats most of the food at dinner, but she's still skinny. She's athletic."

"You look athletic too. Do you two play tennis or anything?"

Walter screwed up his face. "Nah. Not interested. And anyway, Linus has a bit of a candle burning for Clarice." (He has a crush on her.)

"Ah."

"He's actually taking her to lunch tomorrow. But just to the hot dog cart in Paris Park. He figures she can't do too much damage to his wallet there."

"Good thinking." Ronda laid a hand on his arm, and Walter thought he might jump through the ceiling. But he maintained his composure. After all, he wasn't almost sent to a place for juvenile delinquents because he lost his cool. Quite the contrary. Walter can pick a pocket with the best of them, and breaking and entering? No problem.

You can see why his Auntie Max thought he needed a fresh start in the States. Walter did too. He'd grown tired of looking over his shoulder.

And who should enter the kitchen just then but Madrigal Pierce herself, the headmistress of the school. "Why Walter, whatever are you doing here?" She sniffed. "My students don't normally act as kitchen help."

"Just doing it for my friends, ma'am. The Sandwiches needed an extra hand tonight—you can see how popular this party is." *(Walter always knows exactly what to say to smooth things over. This is called being diplomatic.)*

"Ronda, dear," said Madrigal as she sauntered over to the counter in her high heels while adjusting her summer shawl around her shoulders. She, too, was dressed primarily in black—heavens but she'd never actually *costume* herself for one of these events! And with her dark hair, she could have been Ronda's older cousin. But that's where the similarity ends.

Ronda inhaled through her nose, settling herself before speaking, "Yes, Ms. Pierce?"

I did mention that the school tries to be snooty, did I not?

"I hate to criticize ... "

I'll bet you do, thought Walter.

" ... but the punch is a little too sweet for my liking."

Ronda took a pitcher of punch out of the refrigerator, reached for a glass, and filled it three-quarters full. She then cut a lemon in half and squeezed in all of its juice. She handed Madrigal the glass. "Then this should suit you, Ms. Pierce."

Madrigal glared at her and then flounced from the room, leaving the glass of punch behind.

Walter laughed. "Good going, Ronda."

He was in love. Sort of.

Meanwhile, the twins were hard at work downstairs. Ophelia balanced the hors d'oeuvre tray on her palm, while Linus, not exactly a physical genius, clutched his tray with both hands as they walked around listening to many of the guests try pirate speak.

"Oh my goodness," whispered Ophelia, "this is ridiculous."

My costume is what's ridiculous, thought Linus.

"You've got the best costume of the three of us, Linus. I hope you know that. You at least look cool. I look almost matronly." (That means she looks like an older woman.)

They offered plates of seafood and small plastic cups of chowder. The food was definitely an improvement over the last party—the one with a medieval theme and positively medieval food. *I'm rather glad I wasn't invited to that little soiree (pronounced swah-rey, which means "social gathering"). And might I add, the chowder was splendid! Ronda made sure I got a second serving too.*

Uncle Auggie had made himself up as Captain Ahab, and

he'd even fashioned an apparatus around his calf to simulate a wooden leg. *(More like a wooden log—it thumped horribly while he paced the wooden floors of the bookshop. Terribly distracting.)* Meanwhile, Aunt Portia didn't care about the Moby Dick theme at all. She figured it was a water party and mermaids live in water, so it stood to reason that she could fudge a little bit.

"Who's to say there weren't mermaids swimming around the whaling ships?" Portia had asked Ophelia earlier. Ophelia shrugged, silently cursing the fact her costumes were at the whim of her uncle.

Portia sparkled in shades of blue, green, and purple. She looked like the queen of the ocean depths, and her laughter was just as delightful as she mingled with the guests. Ophelia watched, figuring she might learn a thing or two from her aunt because heaven knows her own mother wasn't going to be there for her feminine education. *(Oh no! That would be too much to ask from someone with so great a mind. Butterflies, indeed!)*

Outside in the back garden, the usual photo station was set up for souvenir pictures, and Augustus had roped Linus into building a set that included a piece of deck railing and a ship's steering wheel. Linus set down his now-empty tray and made sure everything was holding up. And of course it was as strong as it had been when he'd screwed in the final screw with his cordless drill, a little gizmo he'd saved up for three months to buy.

At ten o'clock, Uncle Auggie found the trio who by this time had finished passing out all the food and were hanging around Ronda, chatting about incidentals (nothing important) and scrubbing various kitchen surfaces. They were feeling rather good about themselves due to the fact that Ronda didn't treat them like little kids.

"Well, children! Ten o'clock! Time to head up to bed."

Whereas Uncle Augustus ... well, judge for yourself.

"Feel free to read for as long as you like. Walter, back to the school by eleven."

"Yes, sir."

Ophelia knew better than to think that would ever happen. They had big plans, you see.

Up in the attic a few minutes later, and still wearing their Moby Dick garb to make Captain Ahab's transition a bit easier, they played a game of cards and waited for the clock to click over to 11:11 P.M.

And then the real fun would begin.

four

A Real Piece of Work

Or What Happens When a Protagonist Is Antagonistic?

Your protagonist is your hero, basically. Your good guy. Sometimes it's very clear who fills that role in a story. Professor Xavier in X-Men does the job nicely, while his counterpart, Magneto, is a bad guy through and through. Sometimes, however, it's not so clear-cut (obvious). Take Robin Hood, for example, and his "robbing the rich to feed the poor" business. He's still a thief, but we like to give him a pass on that because, well, people need to eat, and he was giving some folks the means to do just that. Ask your parents whether or not this was right or wrong; I'm just telling you what happened.

If the trio had known just how problematic transporting the captain of a New England whaling ship (the *Pequod*) straight off his boat would be—and from the 1800s, to boot—they might not have been so nonchalant (carefree, casual) about bringing him over from Book World into modern-day Real World.

Captain Ahab was, as they say, "large and in charge." As the captain of a ship, he's used to calling all the shots and having people listen and obey. Quasimodo, the hunchback of

Notre Dame and the teens' first visitor from Book World, was very much the opposite. So the children really had no experience concerning a character like Ahab. And let's be realistic, Captain Ahab wasn't used to taking orders from teenagers.

What I'm doing here is creating tension ahead of time, much like reading a book or watching a movie about the sinking of the Titanic. *You know what happens, and it isn't good. And let me tell you, what happens next is* not *good. Now is the time to let the fist of dread settle in your stomach.*

Ophelia, the most likely to know what was in store for the group, opened her copy of *Moby-Dick* to the one portion where Captain Ahab seems to have an ounce of sanity. She laid it in the circle and said, "So I think this spot in the book is our best bet. The *Pequod* has been sailing around in search of Moby Dick, and Captain Ahab is now realizing that he's in danger of sacrificing the lives of his crew for his own personal vendetta."

In other words, Moby Dick (who is a white whale) bit off Captain Ahab's leg, and now the old man wants revenge. Badly. Imagine that you need to stop at a rest area, but the next exit is one hundred miles away. You simply have to get there. You have to do whatever is necessary. That's how strong Captain Ahab's sense of revenge is, how powerful, enabling him to think of little else.

Got it? Good.

"Get him at a soft spot," said Walter who was lying on the floor getting ready to do some sit-ups. (He believes in exercising as you go.) "I like that."

Like that'll last, thought Linus. "I guess it's as good a spot as any," he said aloud.

"Better than any others that I can think of. The man is

crazy." Ophelia plopped down on the blue sofa. "Are you sure we should do this?"

"Yes!" cried Walter.

Linus walked over to the worktable and leaned against it, shoving his hands into his pockets.

Ophelia looked at her watch. "11:08. Three minutes until touchdown."

This was the first time they'd purposely placed a book in the circle. So whatever happened next, they had no one to blame but themselves. But there seemed to be an inevitability about it all (that this was planned for them by a higher power, and they had little choice in the matter).

Ophelia felt her blood begin to zing in her veins. Linus experienced some dread in his stomach, and Walter, looking as cool as ever, felt the heat of anticipation radiate from his chest and on out to his limbs. This was going to be good.

Their breathing quickened when Ophelia said, "One minute." And when she started the countdown from ten seconds, they all held their breath.

"Look!" said Ophelia.

The circle began to glow, the green light almost pulsating as it emanated from the surface of the portal. It changed from blue to green, then yellow to orange, red, pink, and on into violet. Suddenly, white sparks—a glaring white so bright that the threesome had to shield their eyes—flew up as if from nozzles, fountains of white sparks were shooting up from the circle.

When they ceased, the resulting smoke collected and then disappeared with a *snap!*

Then nothing. Oh how heavy the silence after something like that!

In the middle of the circle stood Captain Ahab, commander of the whale ship, *Pequod*. And he looked as if he were about to punch one of them—any of them—right in the nose. He stood tall, proud, his wool coat, tightly fit to his body still glistening with the spray of the sea. His gray beard also held droplets of the salty water that were as dead stones compared to the mad sparkle in his eyes. It was one thing to imagine a crazy captain, and quite another to see one face-to-face!

"Look at that leg," whispered Linus.

"Carved from the jawbone of a whale," Ophelia whispered back as quietly as she could.

Walter stepped into the circle. "Captain Ahab! Welcome aboard the good ship *Seven Hills*!"

"Aboard a ship, you say?" Ahab's face cleared, the anger replaced by confusion. He shook his head, once, twice, three times. "Am I dreaming, lad? Just a moment ago I was bent over the railing of the *Pequod*, gazing out on the South Pacific, I was. There are times when a man gets to the peak of his life, when two roads stand before him—one road to heaven, the other to hades—and fate sweeps a loving hand toward the dark road ..."

And he went on and on and on. This sort of speech is called a soliloquy. *It's as boring as you might imagine.*

Ophelia was happy for the time it stretched out.

Let him rattle on, thought Linus.

Walter's eyes glazed over, but he was smart enough to realize this was a good thing. *A dream world!* he thought. *Exactly what we need him to believe!*

Walter shot a glance at Ophelia and mouthed the word *dream*. She nodded.

Linus saw. He also nodded.

Ahab's eyes began to blaze. "Aye, so true. A man on the precipice of life and death, and which will he choose? Which will he choose, lad?!" He reached out, grabbed Walter by his full shirtsleeves, and shook him slightly. "Now tell me true, boy. Be this a dream?"

"Yes, sir. A dream it is."

This is going to be a nightmare, thought Linus.

Ahab now noticed Linus leaning against the worktable. "Ho, cabin boy! And what name hail you by?"

"Walter, Captain."

"Good lad. Good lad." He looked around, "Now what sort of ship does this claim to be, young tar? (Tar is a nickname for sailor.)

"Looks to me as if you are a trader of sorts. And if this be true, then what manner of goods are you trading?"

Ophelia stepped forward. "I'm Ophelia, Captain Ahab. Welcome aboard the *Seven Hills.*"

"And aren't you a pretty thing, lass? You remind me of my wife, my sweet young wife who's waiting for me back home in Nantucket. I was just thinking about her. She must have looked like you when she was a lass."

"Well, thank you." Ophelia dropped a curtsy. *This might not be so bad after all,* she thought.

Linus dropped his forehead into his hand. *This is going to be a disaster.*

five

Figuring Out What to Do
with a Mad Sea Captain

"Now, listen you well," said Captain Ahab. "Be this a dream or not, I see many an unusual item around me. And what is that piece of furniture there? None the likes of that are found on Nantucket."

"It's a sofa," said Ophelia. "See?" She sat down and bounced a little. "It's soft and comfortable for your ... well, your bottom."

"Aye."

I wonder if he's going to get tired like Quasimodo did! thought Linus.

"Come have a seat." Ophelia patted the spot beside her. "I'm sure you must be exhausted. And you *are* in a dream, so the sooner you get back to it, the sooner you can once more find yourself aboard the *Pequod*—ready to hunt Moby Dick to his death."

"His death! Aye, yes, his death. The white beast of the sea will finally be in my grasp." He clenched his fists. "You are aware of the great white whale? How so? Are you a seafaring lass?" His gaze shifted to Linus. "And what of you, harpooneer? You look like no harpooneer I've ever seen. No.

What island does so pale a youth come from? You look nothing like Queequeg."

"A harpooneer from the *Pequod*," Ophelia quickly explained to the boys.

"I'm from the island of Willis," said Linus, grasping at the only name he could think of, the name of the island where his self-centered parents were at that very moment studying their own four-winged "Moby Dicks." "It's in the South Pacific," he added.

"What?! And how so? I've roamed the seas of the South Pacific for many years, lad, and I've not heard of such an island as you claim—and certainly none peopled with men so pale as you."

"Perhaps you just haven't discovered it yet," said Walter, taking his arm. "Now here, Captain, lie down on this couch—"

"I thought the lass called it a *sofa*."

"Aye. Sofa *and* couch. It's like ship and boat," Walter thought quickly.

Ahab nodded and stroked his beard.

Walter continued, "Now take a rest. Take the mantle of a good night's sleep upon your heavy shoulders, 'tis a weighty matter you bear with the white whale. Rest now, I say. In the morning, you'll awaken and find yourself once more aboard the *Pequod* and on the trail of Moby Dick!" Walter's voice rose with each word he spoke, while Linus and Ophelia just stared at him open-mouthed. *(The British accent helped quite a bit, I might add. Walter seems to prove himself handy again and again.)*

"Aye, lad. Aye, aye, you have yourself a good point there. 'Tis true I need a rest. I haven't slept for days and days. And on the morrow, my mind will be as clear as the mists themselves clear. And then Moby Dick shall be mine!"

Linus rolled his eyes. *We have to stop him from giving speeches. This is getting ridiculous.*

"Will you be my cabin boy—what 'tis your name again?" Ahab asked Walter.

"My name is Walter, sir. And t'would be a pleasure."

T'would? Linus had to admire his friend. He was playing the part with aplomb (assurance).

"Let me help you to bed, Captain Ahab, sir," said Walter. Turning to his friends, he said, "You two may return to your posts now."

"What do you do aboard this ship?" Ahab asked Ophelia.

"I'm the ship's cook! I make a mighty fine chowder, sir."

"I'd like a taste of that someday—if I ever make it back to these waters. Of course, I suppose that will be up to me, considering this is my dream."

"Yes, sir." Ophelia curtsied.

"I never would have considered having a woman cook on a vessel like the *Pequod*, but I suppose I have only myself to blame. Go make us a fine chowder, lass! And if I ever come this way again, I'll drink a bowlful and be thankful to you."

When Linus and Ophelia left the room, Walter settled Captain Ahab on the couch and covered him with the afghan Ophelia kept up there for those times when she wanted to snuggle in and read.

"All right now, Captain. I'll just be lying on the floor over here if you need me."

"Thank you, lad." Ahab closed his eyes and folded his hands across his stomach. "'Tis been a strange day, indeed."

Five minutes later, the captain's soft snore assured Walter that he could check in with the other two.

Ophelia jumped to her feet when Walter entered Linus's bedroom, the trio's other hangout spot. *(Although why they seemed to gravitate toward that space, I cannot say. The boy needs to do laundry a little more often.)*

"You didn't leave him awake and alone, did you?" she cried.

"Of course not. He's asleep. I just came down to get a pillow and blanket. I'll sleep up there on the floor. We can't take any chances with this one."

"He's no Quasimodo," said Linus.

"Good." Ophelia arose from her perch on Linus's blue beanbag chair. "Now I'm going to go online and download a recipe for chowder. I hope Aunt Portia has some canned clams on hand."

She hurried from the room.

"Good thinking on her part," said Walter.

"Can we keep up the whole dream scheme?" asked Linus.

"I don't know if it matters, mate." Walter picked up a sleeve of Saltines lying next to Linus's latest airplane design on his drawing board. He pulled one out. "A man with a personality like Captain Ahab will do what he likes, dream or not. Maybe even more so. After all, we're not real people to him, are we?"

"Great."

"Yeah." Walter munched on a cracker. "What do you think we should do?"

"Get rid of that vendetta (an ongoing, bitter rivalry), for starters."

"I agree. Right. Well, let's think about this. He hunts Moby Dick because the whale took his leg, right?"

"Yep."

Walter plopped into the beanbag chair. "So what if we get him a better leg? I mean, what bloke wants to walk around with a peg-leg made from the jawbone of a whale? It's bloody awful!"

"A real prosthetic?"

"Right. More comfortable, too. And there's a good chance it might soften his bent on revenge a bit."

Linus nodded. "I'm on it."

Ophelia spun around at the sound of her aunt's cough.

"Ophelia, dear! Whatever are you doing? It's midnight and you're cooking?"

Ophelia help up a wooden spoon. "Chowder! I'm making chowder. I was so into my role for the party, I figured I might as well go with it."

"Well, wonderful!" Aunt Portia clapped her hands. "I think it's terrific. Just terrific!" She leaned toward Ophelia. "You *do* realize there's leftover chowder from the party in the refrigerator, don't you?"

Oh my goodness, thought Ophelia, but she said, "Yes, of course I do." *Now.* "I just wanted to try my hand at it."

"Good then, dearie. I'm off to bed. See you bright and early in the morning."

Ophelia shook her head. "Early?"

"Oh, I don't blame you for forgetting." Aunt Portia slid off her mermaid tiara, snagging her frizzy hair in it. "Tomorrow is the town meeting about that cougar. You said you wanted to go."

"Has it attacked again?"

"Just this evening. A small dog over by Paris Park. Father Lou had recently adopted her—a tiny little mutt. She jumped

43

out of his car and took off, presumably right into the cougar's clutches. Isn't that awful?"

"Horrible!"

"Lou is upset, as you might imagine. That man has a heart of gold."

Makes sense after our sighting yesterday, thought Ophelia. "Yes, of course I'll go. Nine o'clock, right?"

"Precisely right. We'll walk over about ten minutes 'til."

I'll just have to leave those boys to deal with Captain Ahab and hope Cato Grubbs doesn't show up to make things difficult, Ophelia thought. Locating Ronda's chowder leftovers in the refrigerator, she eyed the start of her own soup.

"No sense reinventing the wheel (doing something that's already been done)," she muttered. And with that, she lifted the pot off the stove, took it down to the backyard, and set it on the picnic table to cool.

six

A New Limb Solves Everything. Isn't That Right?

*W*alter knew they were in for real trouble when Captain Ahab spat out the peanut butter and jelly sandwich Linus made him for breakfast.

"What is the likes of these victuals (food supplies)?" he roared. His face reddened beneath his bushy gray beard, and his blue eyes blazed like a furnace. "And why am I still here, boy? Was that sleep a dream within a dream? Surely I'd be awake by now and back aboard the *Pequod* ready for today's chase. I have him in my sites, lad. Moby Dick shall soon be mine!"

"This is our usual fare aboard the *Seven Hills*, Captain, and it will give you extra strength for the fight," Walter said soothingly.

Oh, no, thought Walter, *I hope he doesn't go back to being Captain Crazy. Where are you, Linus! And where is that blasted leg!*

"Fetch the cook, my boy! She needs a scolding for offering such food to a hungry man far from his ship."

"Now, now, Captain. Miss Easterday does the best she can aboard our boat. All of the men are most happy—"

He raised an eyebrow and a finger. "Which leads me to ask: Where *is* the rest of the crew? 'Tis a strange boat that I am on, lad. A very strange boat indeed!"

"We're docked now, sir, in Kingscross."

"Along the Bard River? How so? How is a whaling boat docked in so shallow a tributary?"

"Oh, sir! We never claimed to be a whaling boat. We're a simple ..." he searched his brain, "... merchant schooner taking supplies up and down the east coast. Mostly books," he added, hoping against hope that Captain Ahab would be placated (restored to a peaceful state).

"Books?!" he roared again. It seemed he liked to roar. The captain jumped to his ... foot and peg. "How does this dream so beggar the sailing profession with talk of such cargo? What sort of a ship carries books as its primary cargo, lad? Tell me that!"

Now he started pacing, and the rhythmic thumping of the ivory peg-leg resounded against the floor of the attic. *Thump, step. Thump, step.* The sound kept ringing and ringing. If Uncle Augustus were home, what would he think about all that noise?

"The *Seven Hills* does, sir," Walter said as he saluted the pacing man. "Now, just sit back down on the sofa, and I'll fetch Miss Easterday to make you a proper breakfast."

The captain's ire (anger) abated (went away). "I do enjoy this sofa. Could entice a man away from the sea, this kind of comfort." He sat back down, immediately quieting the thumping.

Oh no. I don't even know how to boil water! Walter thought as he hurried down to the kitchen. He rifled through the refrigerator, wondering what people in the 1800s ate for breakfast. Eventually, he came up with some leftover chowder and a cup of shrimp cocktail, complete with spicy dipping sauce.

Meanwhile, Linus had located a prosthesis maker in the phone book and was there now. Walter was on his own.

Linus sat across the desk from Mr. Abner Foltingspeer and tried his best, and with as few words as possible, to get the man to let him take a leg home with him—just for a few days so that a visitor could "give it a try."

"Now, Mr. Easterday, we just don't do things that way. A patient must be measured, you see. I don't even know where the man's leg ends or how many inches long the prosthesis needs to be." Mr. Foltingspeer held the palms of his hands up and shrugged. He really wanted to help, it seemed. Linus figured him for a father of two who actually helped his kids with their homework.

"I took care of that," Linus reassured him. Then he pulled out a sheet of paper containing a quick sketch of Ahab's leg (which he'd done while the old man was sound asleep). "And I measured, too. It needs to be about 16 inches long."

It's good to have at least one scientific sort along when an adventure is in progress.

Mr. Foltingspeer nervously ran a hand over his close-shaved head.

"Please, Mr. Foltingspeer. Just until noon on the fourteenth. I'll have it back by then." *Or will I? Will Captain Ahab insist on taking it back through the circle? Most likely.*

The prosthetist sighed. "All right. I can't guarantee it will be exactly the right length, but we'll try and get it as close as we can. I have a box of discards in the back."

Fifteen minutes later, at 9:35 A.M., Linus walked down the street with a prosthetic leg in his hand.

Ophelia sat on a folding chair in a classroom in the Life Sciences building at Kingscross University, silently praying the guys were all right. If anybody could be alone with Captain Ahab, it would be Walter; and if anybody could procure a prosthetic leg on the fly, it would be Linus. Still, her heart thumped as she wondered how they would contain the sea captain as the hours wore on. The portal travelers, they'd learned from one of Cato Grubbs's notebooks, stayed in the Real World for sixty hours, or until 11:11 A.M. on the third day. She supposed an A.M. had to balance out the P.M.

Now it was just after 10 A.M., which meant they had a little less than fifty hours to go. Two whole days. A biology professor stood behind a podium telling everyone seemingly everything he knew about cougars. The cat probably wouldn't attack human beings. Yes, it was most likely a male cat due to the fact that no other cougars had been spotted. It was safe to assume he roamed here alone and would keep to himself, marking his territory as he went along.

"How will we trap it?" This question came from a frightened woman who lived next door to the rabbit massacre behind the professor of sustainable urban agriculture's house. *(She also happened to have the most shocking yellow hair seen in our little town then, now, or ever.)*

"Well, there are plenty of different traps we could use, but I'm not sure that's the best tactic to employ." The blond professor, who looked more like a male model than the typical nerdy scientist, reached into the inside pocket of his blue blazer and pulled out a baggie filled with a rubber shot. "If we just shoot him in the hindquarters with this, he'll realize the feeding frenzy in Kingscross is over."

Everyone nodded.

"Is it humane?" an older woman sitting in the front row asked.

"Yes. Surely it's uncomfortable, but it's better than being shot with real bullets by someone who's threatened by the cat's presence."

It sounded like a good idea to Ophelia, but what did she know?

Aunt Portia leaned toward her. "I feel a bit sorry for the cougar."

"Me too," Ophelia whispered, looking at her watch and wondering how much longer this could go on.

"Have any of you been feeding the cougar?" the biologist asked.

"Oh yes!" A young woman of the hipster variety said proudly.

"Well then stop it right away!" he scolded. "It has to know the gravy train has left the station."

(Yes, he actually used that expression. I'm not writing a cliché to try to make you feel more at home. I'm just telling you what happened.)

"Well, it better not come onto my property again," a man in overalls said. "It got one of my lambs three days ago."

Ophelia felt sorry for the lamb too.

"As far as I know, the problem is that we don't have a good tracker available to us right now," the mayor of Kingscross said from his place next to the biologist. "So it will be up to you folks to keep us abreast of the cougar's whereabouts. When you see it, call this number right away."

Everyone with pens wrote down the number—including Ophelia.

As Ophelia and her aunt walked back to Seven Hills, she said, "I hope we see the cougar before anybody shoots it."

"As do I, dearie. It is, after all, only being true to its nature."

Everything needs to be true to its nature, Ophelia thought as Captain Ahab's face appeared in her mind.

Walter set the breakfast tray on Captain Ahab's lap.

"Ah, now this is more like it!" He spooned a mouthful of chowder between his lips. "Aye, and so I'm right! This will put flesh on a man's bones and strength in his step, lad. Why a chowder like this will give any man the wherewithal to kill Moby Dick!"

"Aye," said Walter. He was getting a bit tired of Ahab. Moby Dick this. Moby Dick that. Obsessions were fine and all that, but did they have to hear about the white whale all the time?

Captain Ahab picked up a shrimp and bit down. "And this is delicious too. That Miss Easterday of a certainty knows how to use a stove to its fullest capacity, does she not?"

"Put some sauce on it, sir," said Walter. "It's even better that way."

Captain Ahab did. His eyes lit up. "This is delicious! Bring her to me right away, lad. I wish to congratulate her on a job well done."

"She's not aboard right now, sir. She's procuring supplies in town."

"Then let's go, lad! Let's see this town and this river.

I'm getting cabin fever down here. But first, I'll finish my breakfast."

Walter looked up through the trefoil window and saw the clouds in the summer sky. *Please, please, let Linus get home soon.*

seven

What a Crank!

*L*inus rushed up the steps and into the attic, breathless. He needed to take better care of his body. He'd ask Clarice Yardly-Poutsmouth to play tennis with him sometime soon—maybe this afternoon, since their lunch date obviously wasn't going to work out today. She liked sports, he liked her; it seemed like the perfect situation.

"I've got it!" He held up the prosthetic leg.

"Well done, mate!" Walter cried then turned to Captain Ahab. "Look, Captain! There is a man in our fair town who makes legs of a fashion to work like real legs. And they're much more comfortable too, I'll warrant."

I'll warrant? thought Linus.

It looked almost robotic. Walter moved the foot piece. "Feast your eyes on this! Look at that movement." He bent the knee. "Isn't this amazing, sir? Think of the greater balance you'll have on deck now. It will almost be like you're not missing that leg at all, sir."

Captain Ahab set aside the tray. *Some things are even more important to a person than food, no matter how good the food is.* "Aye?" He stepped closer to Linus with a look upon his face that neither boy could understand at their age.

But I can tell you what it was: Amazement and hope mingled together with the fear that maybe this wonderful thing will work for everyone else in the world but you, because you've lived long enough to know that there are always exceptions to the rule, and you've been the exception enough times to know that you can be the exception again.

"What is this?" Captain Ahab asked.

"We call it a 'prosthesis' around here," said Walter. "Look, isn't it fantastic?"

Captain Ahab shook his head as if loosening something tight and stuck inside. "I truly must be dreaming," he whispered. "Where else but a dream could something like this be?"

"Try it on, sir?" Linus held it out.

"Aye, harpooneer. To be sure I will." He sat on the sofa and pulled his pant leg above his knee. He unbuckled the strap that held the piece of ivory to his leg and took it off. Walter and Linus could see that his leg ended just above the knee, the skin folded underneath like living fabric.

"That healed nicely, sir," said Walter. "Considering you had no antibiotics, I'd say you got through that relatively well."

"*Antibiotics*?" Captain Ahab looked at him suspiciously. "What do you mean by that word, son?"

"We have them here in Kingscross, sir. Aye, it is medicine that kills infection making it less likely for people to die when they're wounded profoundly as ye were, sir."

"'Tis the strangest dream I've ever had. How would I even think to dream such wonderful things?" He peered at Linus. "Be you sure I'm in a dream?"

Linus nodded. He hoped lies to fictional characters didn't count.

Walter handed the prosthetic leg to Ahab. "Try it on, sir, and we'll find you a good pair of shoes for your feet, the old one and the new one."

Linus took that as his cue and ran down to the costume room.

When he returned to the attic, Ahab stood with his legs spread wide, hands on hips. "Look here, lad! You'll not believe what, to be sure, is a miracle. A true wonderment! 'Tis true I must be dreaming."

Ahab took one step and then another. He was obviously a man of great coordination, and a man used to keeping his feet secure in places where they're not likely to be kept. Captain Ahab had seen a lot of storms on his voyages, yet he'd managed not to be swept off the deck in all his years at sea. Trying out a newer and better leg in the attic of Seven Hills Better Books was but a trifling (small) matter to someone like the salty sea captain from Nantucket.

Ophelia entered the room. "Oh my!" she said. "Why, Captain Ahab! Look at you, sir. Walking around like you were born with that leg! I can't believe it."

He lifted his leg and shook it, then began singing, "Was you ever in Quebec? Bonnie laddie. Hieland laddie." He stepped to. "Stowing lumber on the deck, bonnie hieland laddie. Way, hey and away we go—" he grabbed Ophelia's hand and she began to whirl with him—"bonnie laddie, hieland laddie! Way, hey and away we go, bonnie, hieland laddie!"

He repeated the song, and soon the rest of them joined in, whirling and dancing. Walter did the occasional somersault, Linus managed something that looked a bit like the Twist, and Ophelia held on to the spinning Ahab like a miser holding his purse. (A miser *is a rich person who refuses to spend* his money on *anything—least likely his relatives, and especially not his son who works in the English department of Kingscross University.)*

"Whoever knew sea captains could be so much fun?" Ophelia gasped, plopping onto the sofa to catch her breath.

Ahab sat down too. "Why, lass, we are the most amusing of the bunch if ye just grant us a bit of time to show off our good natures. We just don't throw them up in the air for all to see."

The boys sat on the floor.

"Sometimes even for years," he continued. "It's the way of life on the sea, young people. It's the way of things when one day you're waiting for one gust of wind to fill your sails, and the next day a storm arises so quickly that you wonder if you'll see your fair sweetheart and child ever again. And you pray that if you die, you'll hit the water and end your life right then before the sharks—"

"What about whaling?" interrupted Linus who knew better than anyone about his sister's squeamishness. *(Quite frankly, Ophelia couldn't stomach even the most ineptly assembled Halloween costumes one sees these days—those disgusting things with fake blood and dirt and grime. And how mothers can allow their children to appear so foul in public, one cannot begin to guess.)*

"Whaling? You want to be hearing about whaling, you sods from a book boat?" He spat out the words *book boat* like pesky gnats. "Well, I cannot fault you there. It's like life aboard many other seagoing vessels a good part of the time. But then something happens, the magic of the whaling boat, when from the lookout somebody yells, 'There she blows!'" He jumped back to his feet. "You see the mist from the blowhole of the whale as it rolls across the ocean depths. And your heart begins to beat like it means it, like it finally got the rhythm it was meant to have, the rhythm of the hunt, the beat of the chase, and you become alive! It feels as if even the hairs on your head are living things ready to get that beautiful whale, ready to jump aboard the harpoon boat and give chase. Even your hairs long to grasp the shaft of the harpoon, sidle up beside the great beast of the sea, and raise the point, ready to—"

"Look at the time!" Linus cried.

Walter, now noticing Ophelia's pale face, took Ahab's arm and said, "Sir, I'm sure you'll be wanting to find a place to ..." He hesitated.

"To what, lad? Speak your mind!"

"Relieve yourself?" He shrugged, winced, even.

"Aye, there's a lad! Lead the way!"

Somehow they managed to get him down the steps and into the bathroom without Aunt Portia hearing them in the bookshop. Uncle Auggie was having lunch with Professor Birdwistell and Ronda over at Father Lou's manse (house) next to the All Souls Episcopal Church across the street. *(Father Lou makes a scrumptious baked ziti. Or so I hear, having never received an invite myself. But then again, I am Presbyterian.)*

As with Quasimodo, the flushing system seemed like a miracle to Captain Ahab. "This changes everything!" he declared. "Show me how this works, harpooneer!" Ahab had already figured out who the technical genius of the trio was. "When I wake up, there will be changes coming aboard the *Pequod*!"

After a quick explanation of water pressure and the S curve of the pipe by Linus, they left Captain Ahab to his privacy.

Back in the attic, Ahab examined the children more closely—one after the other. "Why, to be certain you're wearing the strangest of clothing this day. What happened to your proper garb?"

Walter looked down at his athletic shorts. "This is the way we dress on ... on ..."

"Sunday!" cried Ophelia.

Ahab waved a hand, disgust curling his mouth. "Don't be trying to take me to church. When my leg went, my religion went with it." He leaned forward. "Some people say I've become a denizen of the dark side of the universe. They say I'm in league with the Devil." These last words came out in a raspy whisper.

The trio looked at each other, the seconds wearing on, then burst out laughing.

Ahab sucked in his breath. "You make merry at my expense?" he roared.

Ophelia, whose guilty pleasure could be found in the utter inanity (ridiculousness) of reality television, said, "Oh no, sir! It's just that nowadays—excuse me—*here* in Kingscross, we don't think of people that way."

"Right," said Walter. "We realize there's a little bit of dark in all of us, and every day it's a struggle to overcome it." Walter knew that better than anyone in the room, actually. He thought of all the nice men and women he'd pickpocketed in London over the years and wondered how he'd ever make things right again.

"So that doesn't frighten you?" Captain Ahab asked.

"Nope," said Linus. "Sir."

Ahab raised an eyebrow, scratched his chin, then sat back. "Most mysterious a lot you are."

"I just went down to the bathroom for a minute!" Walter cried. He ran out into the backyard where Ophelia and Linus were weeding Uncle Augustus's vegetable garden.

Ophelia wiped her dirty hands on the front of her jean shorts. *(An act I've never understood, by the way. Isn't it better to wash one's hands in the sink than throw dirt-encrusted denim into the wash and expect it all to come out clean? Goodness, but young people can be so dense when it comes to cleanliness.)*

"What do you mean, Walt?"

"He's gone! Captain Ahab has left the building!"

eight

A Captain Will Sail No Matter What and a Hunter Needs His Prey

*L*inus scrambled to his feet and ran straight through the bookshop and out the front door. The others followed.

"I didn't hear him on the steps. Surely with that leg ..." said Ophelia.

"Too bad we didn't give it to him *after* lunch." Walter looked up and down the street. "No sign of him."

Linus crossed Rickshaw Street and made for the park and the Bard River.

"Good thinking, Linus!" Ophelia struggled to catch up.

All three of them made a beeline *(went in a straight line, not worrying about sidewalks which are put there so children like them don't trample the lovely grass that the parks and recreation people work so hard to maintain)* toward the flowing waters of the river.

Before they got there, however, they heard a familiar voice yell, "Give me your craft, lad! Are you a nincompoop, young man? I'm in need of transport along this river to be certain. Now hand me your ... well, now, I don't quite know what to call that. But it looks seaworthy enough to hold the likes of me." Captain Ahab grabbed hold of a chubby eight-year-old park-goer's inner tube, his hands grasping the black rubber like the pincers of a crab. "Give it to me, I say."

Ahab gave it such a yank, it pulled straight away from the boy, causing him to fall backward on his bottom and leaving him as angry as a hornet. "What do you think you're doing, old man?" he yelled, then let fly a mouthful of insults.

Ahab's eyes widened, and he gazed at the threesome as they dashed up to him. "What in the name of all that's decent has happened to this young lad? It sounds as if his mother has forgotten how to raise her young ones." He leaned down and grabbed the boy's forearm. "I'll not shy away from being the one to teach you a lesson, you belligerent little—"

"No!" Walter pulled Captain Ahab's hand away. "That's not how we do it here, sir! Leave that boy alone unless you be wanting the law after you."

"What nonsense say you, lad? Children are not to speak to their elders with such disrespect. He should go into the stocks right away!"

Ophelia took his arm. "If you hurt somebody else's child here in Kingscross, sir, *you'll* be put in the stocks."

He snatched his arm away. "As if I can believe a word any of you scoundrels say! You told me I was on a boat, and instead I find I'm in the attic of a bookseller. What is the matter with young people who cannot find the truth in their mouths though they look for it with the light of a thousand candles?"

Oh, very nice! thought Linus. *Very poetic, Captain Ahab.*

"That was a beautiful metaphor, sir. We just didn't want you to feel uncomfortable upon your arrival." Ophelia felt the need to curtsy. "We thought you'd bear the transition better if you thought you were somewhere most comfortable to you."

"Why wouldn't I be comfortable? I'm in my own dream, am I not?" He placed a hand atop his head. "Or am I?" He whirled on them, sticking his pointer finger in each one of their faces in turn. "What other lies have you been speaking, children? I saw the strangest carriages speeding along without horses, fountains of water spraying up out of nowhere, and black ropes strung from pole to pole all along the street! Ah, certain and for sure I'd like to know the truth whereof you do not speak—and right now!"

Ophelia sighed. "When we get back to the attic, I'll tell you everything. I promise, sir. But for now, there's someone I'd like you to meet."

"And who would that be?"

"Father Lou, the vicar at All Souls Episcopal Church." She pointed across the park to the steeple. "Right over there."

"I told you, I will *not* be going to church!"

She blushed. "It's not really Sunday."

"Liars! The entire bunch of you are ruffians!" Then he pointed to Linus. "Except for you, lad. You don't say much of anything."

Walter thought, *I wish we could say the same about you, Captain Ahab.*

"There's a good reason for our lies, I promise!" Ophelia bounced on her toes. "Please, sir. You've got to believe us."

Ahab's gaze circled around them. "All right, then. I have to be fair about this. You've given me hearty victuals and a comfortable bed upon which to rest my hoary head. You've given me a fine leg as well. I see you mean me no harm."

"Right!" cried Walter. "Let's go see Father Lou!"

Thankfully, Uncle Augustus had decided to practice on the church's organ after lunch. *(He'd just begun taking lessons, and it was easy to tell that it was he who made such an august (majestic) instrument like the pipe organ sound like an asthmatic cat gagging on a popcorn kernel.)*

Linus knocked on the back door of the manse. Two seconds later, Father Lou, once a motorcycle-riding bounty hunter (someone who brings in wanted criminals) turned man of the cloth (priest), pulled open the door. He raised his brows. "Let me guess. Captain Flint from *Treasure Island*."

"No." Ophelia hugged him and whispered, "Ahab. Only he doesn't know about the nature of the circle yet."

"Aaah." Father Lou held out his hand to the sea captain. "My name is Lou Wellborne, and it's a pleasure to meet you, Captain Ahab."

They shook hands. "You won't want me going into the sanctuary now, will you? For truly, I've sailed to many a place, man, seen many a sight, and heard many a sound, but I've yet to hear what is coming out of that building."

Ophelia stifled a laugh. *Poor Uncle Auggie.*

"Nobody deserves that. How about a nice strong cup of tea?" Father Lou smiled.

"Sure and for certain I haven't had one in a good long time. Why, I'll be pleased to accept your offer and extend you my thanks." He turned to Walter and said about Father Lou, "I like this one's hair. Reminds me of my men."

He was, of course, referring to Father Lou's long white ponytail.

"And, meaning no offense lads and lass, it's good to be around an adult at last, even seeing as he looks like no man of the cloth I've ever seen back on Nantucket. Maybe I'll get some answers."

Father Lou, wearing a pair of jeans and a Harley Davidson shirt, turned from his place at the stove. "All in good time, Captain. My friends here have a whale of a tale to tell you! You're not going to believe it."

As he made the tea, Lou asked Captain Ahab about life on the *Pequod*. *(Naturally he did this after asking what boat he sailed on, what kind of boat it was, and such. He definitely knew how to get with Ophelia's program and not give anything away. Father Lou had street smarts even keener than Walter's.)*

Captain Ahab, having sailed for so many years, gave him only the broadest of descriptions. Cutting off the blubber, boiling it, the vast amount of oil inside a whale's head. He did tell a rousing story of one of the crewmates who fell into a whale's head during the process of extracting the oil.

"So they're really that large? Hard to imagine." Father Lou poured boiling water into the teapot he'd already prepared.

"It's like nothing I can accurately describe," said Ahab. "There you are—out on the broad sea and beneath only the eye of God—and the most magnificent of His creatures is right there in front of you."

"Do you ever feel sorry for the whale?" asked Ophelia. "When it's tied to the side of the ship—a shadow of its former glory?"

Ahab whipped his head around and stared at her. "Are you daft, lass? I was put on earth to hunt these creatures! It brings light to people's houses and a host of other needful things. Of course I don't feel bad."

"Really?"

Uh-oh. Linus noticed the tears beginning to form in the corners of his sister's eyes.

Ahab cocked his head, then reached out and patted her hand. "Oh, all right. While I don't feel sorry for the whale, I do feel thankful sometimes. And I do wonder how it is that God ordained feeble men the likes of me to conquer the height of creation. Now *that* I do not understand, lass. That I cannot comprehend."

Father Lou set the teapot on the table. "I've always wondered about that. We don't hunt whales anymore."

"What?"

"From Kingscross!" Walter shouted. "We don't hunt whales from Kingscross!"

Linus closely examined the violet on his teacup. *Father Lou must be slipping.*

The priest realized his mistake right away. "So Ophelia! Tell me what happened during the meeting about the cougar?"

"Oh, they're going to try to shoot it with rubber bullets and hopefully send it on its way."

Ahab sat up straighter. "A cougar?"

"Yes, sir," said Ophelia, not thinking for a moment about what she was saying. "He's been terrorizing the town."

"*Terrorizing* may be overstating it a bit," said Walter, realizing right away what she'd done.

"He killed my dog!" said Father Lou.

"He's killing small pets and people's rabbits and such." Ophelia glared at the priest.

"And they can't trap him? Hunt him down?" Ahab's eyes began to glow.

Here we go, thought Linus. They were in for it now.

A while later, having finished their tea, Captain Ahab was soliloquizing (pretty much talking to himself) about his need to hunt the whale Moby Dick, the way of a life lived at sea—including his first voyage as a cabin boy—the virtues of harpooneers from the islands, and the oddness of all their tattoos. *(At this point in the conversation, Lou wisely didn't raise up the sleeves of his long-sleeved shirt to share his own tattoos.)*

Suddenly, Uncle Auggie rapped twice on the back door before he breezed right in to the kitchen. "Well, look at this gathering!" he said, delighted. When he saw the captain sitting at the table, he asked, "And who have we here? I'm Augustus Sandwich. Pleased to meet you ... "

"This is my uncle!" Father Lou jumped up from his chair. "Right, Uncle Ahab?" He turned to Ahab and winked.

Ahab looked confused. Ophelia leaned over and whispered. "It's a joke we play on my uncle from time to time."

"Aye! Pleasure to make your acquaintance, Mr. Sandwich!"

The men shook hands.

"We were just leaving!" shouted Walter, truly losing his cool for the first time in weeks. There was no way they were going to keep the sea captain from offering up too much information. "Uncle Ahab is a fine tracker, and we're off to see about that cougar!"

"Let's shove off then!" Captain Ahab jumped up, ready to give all he had to the community cause. At least that's what Walter hoped it looked like and not the typical bloodlust of a born hunter who at that very moment was deprived of his true prey.

Ophelia had the group out the door—with proper goodbyes and thanks, no less—in less than a minute.

"We've got to tell him the truth now," said Linus.

"And it's about time," Ahab agreed.

"Let's get back to the attic." Walter led the way across the street.

"These horseless carriages are amazing things!" Ahab cried at the sight of cars whizzing by. "You'll have to show me how they work as well, harpooneer!"

"Believe me when I say that toilets are much easier to understand," said Walter.

Linus opened the door to the bookshop. "Speak for yourself."

nine

The Truth Will Come Out, but First the Stink Must Come Out

To be quite honest—and I haven't had the fortitude to describe this until now—Captain Ahab stunk to high heaven. He'd been aboard the Pequod for quite some time before his crossing to the Real World, and he smelled like a dead fish that had never worn deodorant a day in its life. Walter, the most persnickety of the threesome about personal hygiene, finally could take it no longer, bless his soul.

Walter pulled Linus aside. "Show him how the tub works, mate. For all of us." He held his nose and pretended he was about to regurgitate. *(Honestly, he didn't have to go quite that far, but his heart was in the right place.)*

Linus nodded and thought, *Hopefully Ophelia will pick out a better outfit for him.*

"I'm going to get some more up-to-date clothing for you, Captain—or should I say, clothing more indicative of the way we dress in Kingscross—"

"Well, I'm not seeing the need for different—"

Linus grabbed his elbow. "Have I got something wonderful to show you, sir."

"Even better than the toilet!" cried Walter.

He ushered Captain Ahab back into the bathroom on the second floor and turned on the hot water tap at the tub.

"Well, blow me down, boy!"

"Just wait, sir." Linus put his hand beneath the flow, beckoning Ahab to do the same.

As the waters began to warm, the captain withdrew his hand. "And blow me down once more. What is this?"

"It's called hot running water. There's a water boiler connect in the basement. And that spigot brings in cold water." He adjusted it. "It's perfect now. Try it, sir."

Captain Ahab thrust his hand under the water stream once again and almost giggled with glee. "Ah, yes. Things will improve quite a bit when I wake up and return to the *Pequod*, or whatever it is that's going on here, lad."

Linus put in the stopper and watched as the tub began to fill. "Most respectfully, Captain, it's time for you to bathe." He pointed to a bar of soap. "For your body." Then he gestured toward the shampoo. "For your hair and beard." Finally, he reached into the linen cabinet for a fresh towel, which he then placed on the counter by the sink. "And this is to dry off when you're done. I'll bring in your clothing."

The speech exhausted him. But thankfully, Captain Ahab was only too eager to try out everything. A warm bath drawn in only minutes. Would miracles never cease?

After the captain's bath was finished and he was dressed in a pair of simple black pants and one of Uncle Augustus's button down dress shirts, Ophelia, having already explained his other clothing was being laundered, showed Ahab to the blue sofa and bade him sit. "I don't know how to convince you that what happened is true, but hopefully this will explain it a little better, sir."

She reached under the sofa and pulled out her copy of *Moby-Dick*. Placing it in his hands, she sighed and shook her head.

"A book about the white whale?" The opposite reaches of his forehead tried to touch in the middle. "I never knew one existed before this!"

"Have you heard of the *Essex*?"

"Of course. Sailed out of Nantucket many a time. Terrible thing that happened to her!"

"What happened?" asked Walter, dropping to do push-ups.

"It was rammed by an angry whale," said Linus.

Ophelia's gaze snapped to her brother.

He shrugged. "I couldn't sleep last night. Research. Internet."

"The ship sank," Ophelia said, "and the survivors roamed the seas in harpoon boats. A few made it to Henderson Island and survived. Many of them died, as you can expect, after floating around on the open sea for so long—95 days, to be exact."

(You have to give Ophelia credit for a memory like that!)

"How they survived is gruesome, and I won't go into all that," she said. "But you can go online and look it up yourself, Walt."

"*Online*?" said Captain Ahab. "What will sitting on a rope do for him?"

"It's another wonderful invention called "the Internet," sir. We'll show you sometime. Anyway, this book, *Moby-Dick*, was inspired by that incident."

"What do you mean *inspired by*?"

"It's a novel, sir. And it's all about you."

He examined the book, front and back. "I don't understand

what you're trying to tell me, lass." His face reddened. "And I'm not sure I like the confusion you're causing in an already muddled situation."

She laid her hand on his arm. "Just read for a bit. You can skip the parts about how a whale ship works. I think you've got that down already. Just see for yourself. And then we'll tell you how you got here." She stood up. "Let's go downstairs, guys, and leave Captain Ahab in peace."

Linus checked his watch. 3:30 P.M. "I've got a date. See ya."

Walter looked over the top of the comic book he was reading on Linus's bed. "Yardly-Poutsmouth?"

"Yep."

Ophelia yawned from her spot on the beanbag chair and laid aside another copy of *Moby-Dick* she took from downstairs. "Have fun. Walt? You hungry?"

"Dying of it."

She rolled out of the chair. "Let's get a snack and see how the Captain of Speeches is doing. He's probably hungry by now, too."

Linus perched a tennis racquet on his shoulder and hurried out of Seven Hills.

"I hope he doesn't start including her in our little group," Walter said as he followed Ophelia down the steps.

"Is she that bad?"

"Not really. She just eats a lot. And she doesn't say much."

"Perfect for Linus."

She walked to the refrigerator and pulled out a bag of pepperoni. "I'm getting a little tired of PB&J."

Walter sighed in relief.

"Cheese?" she asked.

"Every time."

She reached in and picked up a block of Havarti.

Now, I have to applaud Ophelia's taste in cheese. I believe Havarti is the cheese most to be adored, and Ophelia agrees with me. What you must remember is that you might find anything lurking in Aunt Portia and Uncle Augustus's icebox. They bring home the oddest things sometimes. Scrapple. Blubber. Kimchi. Dried bananas. Okra. Vegemite. Havarti was a mild addition to the innards of that fridge—might I suggest that it was even a veritable (very much so) relief for the thing.

She sliced squares of cheese approximating the rounds of the pepperoni and laid the slices on top of round, golden and delicious crackers bearing the name of a cushy hotel. *(I'll be hanged if I'm going to provide a little free advertising for them here. If that poses a problem for you, then take it up with management. Thank you.)*

"Have you ever read *Moby-Dick*?" she asked Walter.

"No. But I basically know the story."

She leaned her hip against the counter and crossed her arms. "I wonder if we can make a difference for our Captain Ahab?"

"We sure did for Quasimodo."

The day after Quasimodo went back through the circle, Ophelia discovered her copy of *The Hunchback of Notre Dame* had been altered. In it, Quasimodo delivered an important message in a piece of dialog near the end to Clopin, King of the Gypsies: "Never underestimate the power of young people who love with full hearts and won't let you fall." Ophelia was delighted to discover upon further reading that Quasi was living with Clopin and his ragtag community, taking care of orphaned children and helping the group get along with less pickpocketing and con games than they had been used to doing. Quasi had also decided not to pursue Esmeralda, but she still managed to waste her life on a man who could never fully love her back.

"You're right, Walt," Ophelia said, and she pushed off the counter and picked up the plate. "Let's see how Captain Ahab is doing."

ten

The Strange Thing about the Truth Is That One Can Choose to Believe It or Not

Captain Ahab appeared as if all the color had been sucked from his face for all eternity.

"This is about me; all my thoughts and my motives. And my men. And how did this Ishmael fellow find out all of this? What kind of wizard is he? I must know!"

"Have a snack, sir." Walter handed him the plate and then sat cross-legged on the floor, hoping food would do its usual trick.

Due to the fact that folks on Nantucket, a host of them being stern Quakers, weren't terribly aware of the art of the novel, Ophelia briefly explained to Ahab how Herman Melville (a writer who once sailed aboard a whale ship) made up the story. In his head. And based it all on what he'd learned at sea about what had happened to Captain Pollard and the *Essex*.

"You see that painted circle on the floor there, sir? That's where you came to us, through that thing. If we place a book inside the circle at 11:11 P.M. on the eleventh day of the month, the character we choose becomes real—just as real as me, or Walter here, or Linus. So don't go thinking you're not real." She reached out and touched him on the knee, then grabbed his hand and placed it on her arm. "You see? Flesh and bone."

"Aye." Captain Ahab's expression was darkened with doubt and not a small share of mistrust. *(Who could blame him?)*

"Now, the bad thing is that we have to make sure you get back in the circle by 11:11 A.M. on the third day, or you'll disintegrate."

"What?" he roared.

"She's not kidding," said Walter, reaching for another pepperoni snack. "You'll fizz away like mist in the morning sun, sir. And supposedly it's quite painful. I don't think you'd want to experience it. Nobody would."

"So what you two scallywags are telling me is that I'm not real in the sense of having actually lived this out, although it feels like I have, and that I have less than two days to live?"

"Oh no!" Ophelia shook her head and told him about Quasimodo and the changes at the end of her copy of *The Hunchback of Notre-Dame*.

He rubbed his bearded chin. "I can change my destiny, then?" His eyes sparked with hope.

"If you'd like to, sir."

"I think I'll keep reading and see what destiny this Melville fellow thought I deserved. Can ye find me the part, lass, where ye brought me into this world? No sense in reading what I already know." He leaned forward. "It's a wonder my men haven't mutinied on me."

"I thought so too."

"So ye've read it? You know my fate?"

"You decide your own fate, Captain Ahab, from here on

out. I'm almost finished reading it. And that's another thing about the circle. I have to finish reading the book before you can go back, and if I don't finish ..."

"Morning mists a burning away," he finished.

"That about describes it."

He ran a hand over his head. "'Tis a strange place to be sure, this is. Now let me see how I get this white whale! Let me read on about how I kill this thing I've hunted for so very long!"

Walter stole a look at Ophelia who returned the book with unemotional eyes. *She doesn't know the ending!* he thought.

Boy, were they in for it now. He didn't want to be around when Captain Ahab found out the truth.

eleven

Even Mad Sea Captains Enjoy Some Quiet Reading Time, So What's *Your* Excuse?

Thankfully, Captain Ahab wasn't the speediest of readers. The afternoon had dulled down beneath a thick layer of gray clouds that hovered like a blanket. *(That "hovered like a blanket" bit is another one of those clichés I told you about earlier. I'm sure the sky has been compared to a blanket at least a million times by now.)* Ophelia could see Linus through her bedroom window, and he was getting a good trouncing on the tennis court by Clarice. Walter had decided to play a quick pick-up basketball game over at the park.

Captain Ahab, reading quietly on her bed, was nothing short of a relief. She did hope he picked up the pace so they could discuss the ending, which she was working toward herself.

"I'm going to make us a cup of tea, Captain." Ophelia set down her copy atop her assigned summer reading for school: *The Three Musketeers.* Too bad Captain Ahab couldn't get together with the Countess de Winter. There was no way one could outdo the other in terms of pursuing their desires!

"Thank you, lass," he sighed. "Did I seem that mad to you when I came through the circle?" he asked.

"No. You were tired. I think there's something about our realm that calms book characters a little. Maybe the journey takes its toll on you." She shrugged. "I don't know."

His gaze returned to the pages, and his shoulders sagged toward the floor. Ophelia had never seen a man so sad. Her heart ached for him. She'd have to cheer him up somehow. Plain and simple.

Ophelia set out Aunt Portia's pottery teapot. Then she did what she never thought she'd do, something she normally would have relegated to other braver individuals, people with a higher level of derring-do (heroic daring) than she had.

Ophelia climbed on top of the kitchen counter, opened the highest cabinet, and gripped Uncle Augustus's precious tin of Scottish shortbread. She could barely breathe and prayed a fervent prayer that she wouldn't drop the tin. She imagined the box clattering loudly against the counter and then dropping to the floor—an explosion of cookies and crumbs! *(Oh heavens, Ophelia, don't let that happen! Civilization as we know it might end!)*

Most people have something in their life with which they are so entirely selfish as to become tyrannical. For instance, my mother insisted on drinking a glass of grapefruit juice every night, and woe to any of us who dared finish the grapefruit juice during the day without telling her! The ire resultant made anything Captain Ahab might dish out seem like but a puff of air in the midst of a typhoon.

For Uncle Augustus, it was his cookies. He special ordered them from Scotland—and they weren't that typical brand one always sees at Christmastime. (I'm not saying I wouldn't eat one if you offered it to me, providing you also gave me a wet wipe for afterward. They can be quite greasy, you know.) And he then metered them out: two cookies a day with a cup of Arab coffee from the Mediterranean restaurant near campus. (They don't mind that he brings his own sweets, nor should they at $5 a cup!)

Now Uncle Augustus had never said a word to Ophelia about the cookies. Aunt Portia spilled the news on that one, and suffice it to say that Portia hasn't pilfered (taken one without asking) any cookies since he locked her out of the house for an entire day back in 1986.

However, if you'd seen the look on Captain Ahab's face, the very expression that broke Ophelia's heart, I daresay you would have taken your chances as well.

She placed several cookies (four, to be exact, in the hope that her uncle would figure for a miscount) on a fine china plate that once belonged to her great-grandmother when the family lived an exotic life in Indiana. After that, she sliced up a peach and set three cubes of Havarti cheese with it.

When she returned to her room and set the tray by Ahab, he began to cry. *(Oh dear. So much for cheering somebody up! Ophelia failed miserably at that one, did she not?)*

Ophelia quickly glanced around the room searching for something, anything, that might distract the weepy sea captain.

The computer! Yes! Perhaps with his verbosity (nonstop talking) the Internet would be a fine outlet for him. It might keep him inside the house, too, and that would make their job so much easier.

Shushing him gently like a sister to her little brother, she pulled him from his tears with a cookie *(yes, they are that delicious)* and introduced, or should I say, *unleashed* Captain Ahab on the World Wide Web.

Oh dear.

Linus said good-bye to Clarice, so enamored of the graceful movements on her slender body, the way her blonde ponytail bounced when she ran, and the lovely expression on her freckled face when she looked at him, he became a stammering mess. Barely more than ten words were said between them the entire date, but he did notice they'd worn the same color shorts and liked the same brand of tennis shoe. Despite the awkward good-bye, he felt things had progressed nicely.

He now stood in the attic laboratory, vials and beakers and books and powders all before him in array. Could he find the secret to the circle? Could he figure out how to bring the characters to Real World another way? Or even better—could Linus figure out how to travel into Book World like Cato Grubbs was doing?

And speaking of Cato Grubbs, Linus had noticed something else. Ahab's old ivory pegleg was gone! And in its place was a note written in decorated script *(not too surprising given how fancy a man Cato Grubbs is)*: "Round two, Children! Good luck getting this one back in the circle!"

Linus grinned. So Cato was up to his old tricks once more, procuring literary items and selling them. He tried as much with Esmeralda's emerald necklace. It must have made for a lucrative living indeed.

twelve

When All Else Fails, Hop on the Internet

When Linus entered Ophelia's bedroom, Captain Ahab had already alienated five people in the comments section of *Whales* magazine's website.

Ahab shook his fist at the screen and shouted, "To the devil with ye *a-circle dolphin lover*!"

Ophelia rushed to Linus's side. "So far, even with the hunt and peck system of typing, he's managed to compose ten written essays in the comments section of three websites, and he's wondering why he's being lambasted (berated harshly) by people."

Linus shook his head and smiled. "Ya gotta admit, it's pretty funny."

She nodded, whispering, "I know. Actually, I've been enjoying watching him. He learned how to navigate the Web really easily. When I used the word *navigate* I think it gave him the psychological edge he needed to learn."

"He does explore the open sea," Linus said. "And he seems fascinated by technology."

"True. There must be a certain capable curiosity to a man like Captain Ahab. Anyway, it should be a piece of cake keeping him here until the circle opens."

Linus hoped so, but he knew a lot could happen in forty-three hours.

Including chores. Abominable, miserable, slimy, disgusting chores. Now you may think the life the twins lead is a hoot a minute, roaming around the town, experiencing intrigue from the circle, two eccentric and sometime clueless old people as their guardians, and a terrific best friend in Walter. But there's one thing about their life that's just like yours. They're expected to contribute to the household. Uncle Augustus makes sure of it. He's definitely the villain of chores.

Uncle Auggie entered Ophelia's room just as Captain Ahab shouted yet again at the computer screen.

"Uncle Ahab!" Augustus cried. "What brings you over here?"

Engrossed in his Internet surfing, Ahab just waved a hand and dismissed the greeting.

Augustus shook his head and revolved his left pointer finger around his ear. The twins nodded.

"He just came over to surf the Internet," said Ophelia. "What's up, Uncle Auggie?"

He held up a wire brush and a scrub bucket. "I just bought a large selection of books at an estate sale. It's time to scrub the basement once more. Aunt Portia needs to re-shelve everything after that flood."

Ahab whirled around in the desk chair. "Aye! Swabbing the deck, eh? Good. What flood are you speaking of, old man?"

Ophelia explained about the flash flood that had come through Rickshaw Street a month before, purposely leaving out the part of the story where Quasimodo rang the church bells in warning. No use in giving the captain any ideas about leaving the bookshop again.

"Oh. Well, then. Be good and obey your uncle. I'm trying to convince a host of people that whale blubber is a perfectly acceptable—"

"All right, let's go!" Ophelia grabbed the supplies from her uncle's grasp, snaked an arm through his, and deftly led him out of the bedroom. Linus followed and closed the door in their wake.

I could go into further detail and tell you about the cleaning session down in the nether (lower) parts of Seven Hills Better Books. I could tell you all about the mold, the smell of leftover mildew from all of the books, and the basement flotsam (trash that floated in on the floodwater) that had already been removed. I could even tell you about a crack in the wall where beetles were doing their business, in and out. But that would be absolutely disgusting, and I have a real aversion to loathsome events such as this.

Now *keeping* something clean is another matter altogether!

Suffice it to say that it was not a job you'd want, and by the time they emerged from the basement, they were covered in filth. Ophelia went to her room to get some clean clothing to change into after her very necessary shower, only to find that Captain Ahab had decided that surfing the wide waters of the Web *(bet you didn't know what "www" stood for, did you?)* wasn't that interesting anymore.

"Oh no, he's gone again!" Ophelia wiped a grimy hand across her sweaty forehead.

Linus ran upstairs to the attic. No human life present.

He ran back down. "He's not upstairs, either."

They checked the rest of the house, hoping and praying he hadn't come across Aunt Portia. She wouldn't be as easy to dupe (fool) as Uncle Augustus. Portia seems a bit more flighty than her brother; but actually, she's less apt to believe what she wants to believe, and more likely to see the truth of the matter. Uncle Augustus, on the other hand, likes his world as he likes it, and all the elements of human living become whatever he wants them to be. *(Perhaps you know people like that as well, people who can convince themselves of practically anything. I hope you aren't one of them. You're annoying, if that's the case, and nobody wants to be annoying.)*

The bathroom was empty, although there were signs someone had taken a bath, and Linus found a lone button that had fallen off Ahab's shirt. The kitchen sink held two bowls of chowder. Uncle Augustus must have warmed some and shared it with the captain.

What did they talk about? Linus wondered. *And did Uncle Auggie conclude that "Uncle Ahab" is simply mad?*

The bookshop held no one. Not even Aunt Portia, thank goodness, and they already knew the captain hadn't ventured to the basement.

"Go get Walt while I take the fastest shower of my life," Ophelia said, climbing the stairs two at a time.

Linus saluted and headed toward the secret passage that led from Seven Hills into the Pierce School for Young People. (At one time the mansion had belonged to the family of Madrigal Pierce, the school's headmistress.) He pulled out a piece of paneling from the wall near the tub, got down on his hands and knees, and then stood up again. Wondering how Walter could come through a passageway that gave him the creeps gave Linus a new bit of respect for the wily (crafty) Brit. Just then, a raccoon scuttled by.

A raccoon?

Apparently Madrigal Pierce had pests of greater shape and size than the garden variety field mouse. He'd get Ophelia to mention it to Madge (Walter's nickname for his head-mistress). His sister would get a kick out of that.

Once he'd made his way through the passageway, Linus opened a hidden door in the school's cleaning supplies closet, then made his way down the hall and up the steps to the boy's dormitory floor. After a little knock and the appropriate response, he entered the room. Walter set his book aside. He was reading *Moby-Dick*.

Linus pointed to it. "Popular book these days."

"It's fascinating!" Walter sat up. "It seems everything you want to know about 19th century whaling is all there! And in great detail. Why people call this boring, I don't know."

"Ophelia thinks it's a snooze."

"She's reading it to find out what happens next. That's why some people read," said Walter. "I read to find out things as well. You'd do well to read this too, Linus. Absolutely fascinating! Brilliant!"

And what you just read is one of the reasons why Moby-Dick *is considered a great work of literature. Some people just like to be in the know, and they're willing to read many pages in order to do so. You have to respect that kind of commitment.*

"Ahab is gone," Linus said.

Walter jumped up. "Any idea where?"

"Nope."

"Where was he last seen?"

"On Ophelia's computer."

"Let's go."

Walter moved the computer mouse to remove the screen-saver. He scanned the webpage. Somehow Ahab had found the local paper's website. "There it is!" He pointed to the most recent headline: COUGAR FINDS CHICKEN DELICIOUS.

The boys read the article.

"Roy Mason. He has a hobby farm on the edge of town." Linus had gone there a week before to pick up some home-made strawberry jam for Aunt Portia. Roy was a real reader. They bartered (traded) books for jam, produce, or eggs.

Linus shook his head. "The man loves his chickens."

"He must be devastated," said Walter. "Well, I think we know where Ahab is, mate. And I believe it's safe to assume that if he's not on the hunt yet, he will be at any moment."

thirteen

Could There Be Any More Annoying Adults in One Chapter?

*R*oy Mason the hobby farmer scratched his cheek with his thumb. Before he bought his five acres, he'd worked as an advertising executive in New York City. He knew how to get products to project an image, and he could perform the same magic on himself. Roy grew up in suburban Baltimore, but he looked more like a farmer than most farmers did. He took off his straw hat and rubbed a hand over his thick, wavy hair with rivers of silver running through it.

His tear-filled eyes, however, were as genuine as the fact that his beloved chickens were indeed dead. "Oh, my poor ladies." He sniffed. "I always called them the 'ladies.'" He teared up again.

Ophelia felt her heart break for Roy.

She sure is an empathetic soul. This means she's more likely to feel what other people are feeling than, say, a professor who doesn't care why a student is absent from class. Even if the student decided to paint his mother's kitchen table inside the garage, forgot to open the garage door, and passed out from the fumes. No, even then they count a person absent and dock his grade. People like that professor are called aloof, uncaring, unkind, and lacking in basic human sympathy. And I'm not going to mention any names here, but I suggest you sign up for any teacher other than Dr. Coffee when you register for Intro to Psychology.

"I'm so sorry," Ophelia said to Roy. "You must be so sad."

"I am. Especially about Parma Jean. She was a great little chicken. They all gave us such good eggs."

Walter tried to shake his head as mournfully as possible. Linus wondered how often a hen lays an egg in the first place. Every day? Every other?

"I don't mean to cut short your sorrow, Mr. Mason, but did you happen to see an older gentleman around here in the last hour or so?"

Roy placed his hat back on its perch. "I did. As you say, it was about an hour ago. Strangest thing. He was dressed like a sea captain, and he asked me some questions about the cougar. He had a quaint way of talking, too. I told him the big cat most likely came from the woods over there—" he pointed to the timber behind his small barn "—and probably returned that way. The man then hurried off into the woods."

With many thanks, the trio continued on their way.

As you might guess, not a single one of them knew how to track a person or an animal. To a real tracker or some kind of wilderness guide, the signs would have been obvious. There was a slight drag to the prosthetic leg that damaged the grasses and scattered the fallen leaves, leaving comet tails behind in the pebbles. But these three didn't notice those things. And it's probably because they chose the wrong way to begin with. They should have gone straight back the way both Ahab and the cougar went.

Captain Ahab was a born hunter, and he barely needed any signs. He could feel the cat. He wanted that cat, and he let his feet carry him where they would.

The gang sat around Father Lou's kitchen table. The scruffy priest had just pulled a baking sheet full of peach tarts out of the oven, and the tea was steeping. "He'll most likely be back. And make no mistake, he'll find his own way."

Linus wondered how Ahab had found the farm in the first place and how he didn't get hit by a car on the way there.

"I don't know how he managed to get there at all," said Ophelia.

Walter stuck his fork in his tart. "So what do we do in the meantime?"

"Enjoy the break!"

Ophelia's brow, drawn in concern, suddenly smoothed. "Well, why not? I mean, he might end up as cat food, or he could expose the enchanted circle; but there's nothing we can do about that now, is there? I'm headed back to the house to wrap up *Moby-Dick*."

They finished their tea and then Father Lou shooed them out so he could work on his sermon before his motorcycle club went on a ride. Ophelia hurried across the street.

Walter stepped off the curb. "So, Linus, how about taking a bit of a walk? I've got a shoe that needs repairing, and I thought we could head back to Jack's shoe repair shop."

"Why not?" Linus shrugged.

"Oh the excitement in your voice is blowing me over."

They headed into the school building so Walt could get his shoes, when who should happen to be crossing the foyer but Madrigal herself.

Oh, Madge, thought Linus. He couldn't even begin to imagine how much this pretentious (showy), snooty, blue-blooded yet frayed-around-the-edges fifty-year-old woman *(don't ask how I know her age, it's none of your business)* would loathe such a moniker (nickname). And that just made it all the more fun to use—even if was only in his head.

"Boys! Where do you think you're going?"

"Up to my room, Miss Pierce."

"You know you need permission to take someone up to the dormitory floors, Walter."

"Sorry. I just assumed that because it's summer and because Clarice and I are the only residents right now, rules like that would be suspended."

She tightened her black, fringed shawl around her shoulders and tapped the toe of her high-heeled black shoe. *(It was a very beautiful shoe on a very beautiful foot. But if you tell her I said that, I shall deny every word.)* "Well, you assumed incorrectly."

"Okay, I'll just get my shoes and come back downstairs."

Linus knew he was in for it.

"So, have a seat." Madrigal pointed to a very uncomfortable-looking, wood-framed, old sofa. *(Say what you will about the beauty of antiques, but every single sofa made before 1930 should be thrown on the pyre [heap of wood] and burned until only ashes remain—they're that unworthy of a human backside. Linus thought so, too.)*

Madrigal Pierce perched on the edge of the sofa. "What's your sister reading these days?"

Linus felt relief blow through him. A grilling was coming to be sure, but he wasn't the one to be cooked this time. "*Moby-Dick.*"

"*Moby-Dick*, what?"

"*Moby-Dick*, ma'am." Did he really have to say it twice? How annoying.

"I'll have to talk with her about it. See if she's a fan or not."

Linus wasn't giving up any information.

Madrigal crossed her legs. "Anyway, I saw you two last week—out in the park after midnight. I've a good mind to tell your aunt and uncle that you're sneaking out."

Linus tried his best to give her a blank stare. The truth was, a meteor shower had danced across the sky that night, and they'd had their guardians' full blessing to watch it—not that Madge needed to know that. Linus keeps his cards close to the vest, which means he tells people only what he must.

Madrigal cleared her throat. "Well. Now let me ask you a question. Math—you're good at it, are you not? I'd like to give you a test to see just how good you are. Would you be willing to do that next week?"

Linus nodded. It actually sounded like fun. (*Yes, he is one of* those *people.*)

"Ready to go?" Walter asked as he slid down the banister (handrail) of the main staircase.

"Walter. Please don't do that," Madrigal said.

Walt flashed Madrigal such a winning smile and an easy wink, she blushed.

"Please don't do that once school starts," she amended (rephrased).

As they tromped down the front steps of the school, Linus said, "I don't know how you do it, Walt."

"Neither do I, mate. I just go with the flow."

fourteen

The Arrival of Starbuck—the Man, Not the Coffee

They arrived at Mr. Pine's Shoe Repair minutes before Jack, the owner whose last name isn't Pine, was set to close up shop.

Walter handed Jack the shoes—a pair of loafers for school. "They just need new heels, I think."

Like most American young people, Linus asked himself why Walter didn't just buy a new pair of loafers rather than wasting time getting them repaired. But while Linus and Ophelia weren't exactly rich, they certainly had more funds at their disposal than Walter did. His Auntie Max may have been paying for his schooling, but pocket money was up to his mother. And she didn't make that much. London was an expensive place to live.

Jack examined the shoes. "Yep. You're right. When do you need them by?"

"Take your time. They're for school."

Jack, who reminded the boys of a Siberian husky with his light-blue eyes, grey beard, and great black eyebrows, wrote up the ticket and handed Walter his portion.

"By the way," he said, "that man you were looking for the last time you were in here ..."

(Cato Grubbs, mad scientist at large.)

"You've seen him?" Walter asked.

"Sure did! He came in here yesterday with a pair of boots. He had the funniest-looking guy with him, too. Looked like a sailor. The older man called him 'Starbuck.' It would stink to have a name like that nowadays."

The boys thanked Jack and took their leave.

"I knew Cato was back!" said Linus. "The ivory peg-leg is gone."

"Captain Ahab's peg-leg. Now that would fetch a tidy price, wouldn't it? And he's got Starbuck with him! That's very interesting indeed." Walter pressed the button at the crosswalk.

They headed back down the hill toward Rickshaw Street. "Who's Starbuck?" asked Linus.

"You need to read something other than science and engineering magazines, mate."

Linus shook his head. "I don't think so."

"Starbuck is Captain Ahab's first mate."

"Why do you think Cato brought Starbuck to Real World?" Linus asked. "Cato must know something."

Uncle Augustus and Captain Ahab sat on the front steps of the bookshop, and neither one of them looked very happy.

"Either this man is totally off his nut, or you've got a lot of explaining to do," Augustus said to the boys.

"Aye! This fellow here has been accusing me of lunacy ever since he found me at the park." He lowered his voice and said, "I almost had that cougar in my sites, blast him."

He sat up straighter. "I've tried to tell him who I am with all sincerity—"

"Hmmph. The captain of the *Pequod*. Now, I'm a pretty fanciful person, but this beats all. I'm thinking we need to get this man to the hospital. Of course, Father Lou isn't home right now, so the responsibility is ours."

"Do you see what I mean?" Captain Ahab rose to his feet. "I'm heading back upstairs."

"What do you mean?" said Uncle Augustus.

"It's where I'm staying!"

Uncle Augustus glared at Linus. "Why is he staying here when Lou has perfectly good quarters?"

Think, Linus!

"He's allergic to wool!" Walter cried. "And all of the carpets in the manse are wool! So when Ophelia realized he needed a place to stay, she offered to let him stay here."

"And why wasn't I consulted?"

Linus shrugged. "Because you're a good person. We didn't think you'd mind."

"How much longer is he visiting?"

"He's leaving around eleven in the morning, the day after tomorrow," said Walter.

"All right then. You all just behave yourselves. Ronda said the way his eyes blaze frightens her."

Uncle Augustus tramped inside the store.

Linus turned to Captain Ahab. "Ronda?"

"She came into the house and heated up some bowls of chowder for us. A fairer woman I've yet to see! And kind-hearted too."

Walter sat down and blew a sigh of relief. "I don't suppose it would be too much to ask you to just act normal, would it, Captain Ahab?"

"What's *normal*, lad?"

This is a question that everyone should ask himself at least once a day if he has any hope of making a name for himself or leaving his mark on society. "Normal" people—those who don't make waves or risk having the people begin to wonder about them—rarely do anything to improve society. So if you're one of the oddballs at your school, then you have a much-improved chance of actually doing something with your life. But if all you do is care about what everybody else thinks? Well, you're wasting your energy, and I haven't much to say to you.

"I'm not sure. But what *isn't* normal is talking about being on a whaling ship here in the present," said Walter. "We don't do that sort of thing anymore."

"A truer word was never spoken." Captain Ahab shook his head sadly. "Just read what people have written on that lighted box. Did we really almost decimate (destroy a great number of) the whale population? Did it really come to that?"

Linus and Walter nodded.

"We're afraid so," said Walter.

"Well, one more whale won't make a difference then. In less than two days, I'll be on the hunt once again for Moby Dick!"

Somehow, Walter convinced Captain Ahab to stay put for just a little while. "See here, Captain. I just read that the cougar struck again. This time he was right near an elementary school, and he took a Dachshund from the yard of one of the houses near the baseball field."

"Baseball field?" he asked.

"I could explain it, but I'll show you instead. We've got

chores to do first, but after that, we'll head out to see what we can find. Ophelia? Can I talk to you privately?"

A minute later the trio gathered in Linus's room.

"Tell us about Starbuck." Linus picked up a model airplane.

"He's the first mate on the *Pequod*."

"We know that," said Walter. "What I'm trying to figure out is what reason he might have to come looking for Ahab."

"He's here?" Her eyes rounded.

Linus nodded.

She thought for a moment "Oh yes! He certainly would want to come over."

"So?" Linus asked.

"Well, Starbuck is sane. He sees where this whole thing is going. The crew is wary of Captain Ahab—not that you can blame them. You see, they're supposed to get a portion of the money that's made from selling the whale oil, and Captain Ahab couldn't care less about that now. So the crew spends two years of their lives out on the sea and then comes back with little to support themselves and their families? That's simply unacceptable."

"It isn't any wonder they're upset," said Walter.

"I know! I'm surprised they didn't mutiny months ago. It shows what a fearsome person Captain Ahab can be."

Fearsome? thought Linus.

Ophelia continued. "And if Starbuck came from about the same part of the book as Ahab, then he's seen Captain Ahab staying up for days now, not sleeping, and just looking out over the ocean."

"No wonder he was tired when he first came through the circle." Walter laced his fingers together and cracked his knuckles.

"So Cato needs to keep Captain Ahab here to make sure the captain doesn't get back inside the circle on time. Then Starbuck can take control of the *Pequod*, and the chance of a successful voyage is dramatically increased."

"Makes sense," said Linus. "But why does Cato care whether or not the *Pequod* makes it back or not?"

"Right," said Walter. "Unless … "

"Unless what?"

"There's something else he can bring back if the crew returns with a hold full of whale oil."

"I'll bet he's wheeling and dealing with Starbuck!" Ophelia cried. "I'll bet they've agreed between the two of them that he'll get some percentage of the take, maybe even Captain Ahab's, if the *Pequod* makes safe harbor in Nantucket!"

"What good would that do him?" asked Linus.

Ophelia grinned deviously. "Scrimshaw! He's going to buy up a load of scrimshaw and bring it back to sell!"

Linus had to admit it was a good theory. Scrimshaw, ivory with carved drawings on its surface, and antique scrimshaw probably sold for a pretty penny nowadays.

"But can't he go in and out of books at will?" asked Walter.

Ophelia nodded. "It doesn't make sense. I wish we could ask him."

"And of course, Cato Grubbs is only around when you don't want him to be," Walter said.

"Don't worry," said Linus. "He'll be back."

"And by the way, I finished reading the book." Ophelia's tone became more sober than a member of the Women's Christian Temperance Union. *(Look it up.)*

Ophelia continued, "Unless we can get Captain Ahab to

change his ways and drop his vendetta against Moby Dick, we may just want to keep him out of the circle ourselves."

"That bad?" asked Linus.
"Worse."
When Linus heard the ending, he shuddered. This was serious.

fifteen

Crazy Is as Crazy Does, but Who Wants to Admit They're Crazy?

The trio realized that understanding someone as compli-cated and obsessed as Captain Ahab would most likely come around by talking to someone who could relate to the headstrong sea captain.

"Who do we know that's obsessed with something? Who has wrapped his or her entire life around one thing and one thing only?" asked Ophelia.

It was six in the evening. They'd placated Captain Ahab with a large bowl of chowder, classical music, and some of Linus's engineering magazines. None of them had ever met a person like Ahab before, and while I'm sure there *are* people out there the likes of Captain Ahab, thankfully they are few and far between. And even more thankfully, we don't meet them every day.

"What about Aunt Portia?" asked Linus.

Ophelia raised her eyebrows in delight. "Why didn't I think of her before?" she asked, bopping herself on the fore-head with the heel of her hand. "She's loved books all of her life! She created this bookstore. And when most of her books were ruined in the flood, she sat right down and went about finding more! Talk about a woman with an obsession. That's brilliant, Linus!"

"Absolutely brilliant," echoed Walter.

"But will she believe us?" Ophelia wondered. "I mean, Father Lou did, but he had Quasimodo sitting before him. There's no way Quasi could have been anyone other than that character. As far as Aunt Portia knows, Captain Ahab could be just some crazy old man who went off his medication and is suffering from delusions of grandeur."

Delusions of grandeur come when people think they're Jesus or Mahatma Gandhi, or even when they believe they deserve to be famous someday—and will be—when in reality, they have nothing to show for themselves, no great accomplishments, just the ability to be so absurdly silly that fools

think they're interesting. Athletes can experience delusions of grandeur as well. Just because he's the star of Run of the Mill High School's football team, he thinks he's destined for the NFL. I see those types in the hallways of Kingscross University all the time. But by the time they're seniors, the bubble has usually burst.

"There's no help for it," said Walter. "We simply have to try. I hate to think of Captain Ahab—even as mad as he is—fizzling down to nothing so painfully."

"Me too," said Ophelia mournfully.

Linus, on the other hand, briefly considered the idea that it might not be so bad to witness the consequences of improper use of the circle. Of course, he was humane enough to shove that thought right down and join the others in the general consensus. But still, a fellow couldn't help being curious, could he? *(Of course, none of them considered what kind of putrid mess it all might leave behind.)*

"But in the meantime," said Walter. "I think we need to find Cato Grubbs and get him on our side."

That would be a first, thought Linus.

"I think we're going to find that no two adventures are even remotely alike," Ophelia said. "I'll go talk to Aunt Portia. It would be better coming from me, since I read the classics." She stood and shot a pointed look at Linus.

Linus and Walter sighed with relief.

Ophelia hurried out to find her aunt.

Walter dropped and did some push-ups, while Linus went to Ophelia's room to check on Captain Ahab. The old man had fallen asleep at the computer desk. Linus's heart saddened.

People often accuse scientific types of not having much

emotion tucked inside of them, but that isn't the case. Some people, like Linus, simply can't find a way to express themselves that doesn't make them feel silly or even absurd.

The best thing to do would be to let Ahab sleep, even if it meant that one of them had to stay up all night to make sure Cato and Starbuck didn't get to him.

Linus returned to his room. "He fell asleep."

"Brilliant. Maybe we can get our thoughts straight." Walter started pacing, which reminded Linus of Sherlock Holmes. "So, we really don't want the captain to painfully fizzle away, but we also don't want his crew to go through that terrible ending. In that case, the only thing to do is convince him to change course."

No pun intended, thought Linus.

"So," Walter continued, "we must enlist Aunt Portia's help—and we have no idea if she'll be fully on board—"

No pun intended, thought Linus again.

"—to convince Captain Ahab to think about his crew and give him the real scoop on Moby Dick."

Nobody had bothered to tell Linus the ending of the story. He had a lot of theories, and none of them were bright and happy: The *Pequod* goes down, and the crew is left to survive the horrors of months spent in a lifeboat. The *Pequod* goes down, and they all die. The *Pequod* survives, but so does Moby Dick; thus, the book ends with the reader thinking that those men will be hunting that blasted white whale for the rest of their lives. Actually, maybe the *Pequod* goes down and the men are *still* forced to hunt the whale, but for all eternity—sort of a Davy Jones's locker arrangement (the sailors' name for the bottom of the sea).

Instead of speculating about it any further, Linus asked Walter to give him the rundown.

Walter did. It took two seconds.

Linus let out a long, low whistle. "Maybe watching the movie will help."

"We'll try that tonight," said Walter. "I wouldn't mind seeing it. I suppose when people can actually *see* the error of their ways, there's a good chance for change."

"Not always."

"I wish you weren't right about that. I'm hungry."

"Me too."

A few minutes later they were standing in the kitchen making PB&J sandwiches (with strawberry jam, compliments of Hobby Farmer Roy) when Walter said, "But if none of those work ..."

"Why not throw him back in, though?" asked Linus. "The book has been ending that way for well over a hundred years. What difference will it really make?"

"It will make a difference to the people in that copy of the book. I don't pretend to understand the physics of it, mate. All I know is that we're responsible now to do right by as many people as possible, including Captain Ahab."

A moral dilemma? Linus could hardly believe it was coming down to that.

A moral dilemma occurs when no matter what you do, someone will get hurt. It can also be called a "Catch-22," an expression that came into our nation's colloquial (ordinary, informal) vocabulary upon the publication of Joseph Heller's novel by the same name. I enjoyed the book, of course. You might be required to read it in college if you major in English, which you should. That is, unless you're a dullard; in which case, I say, please do not darken the doors of our department.

Walter picked up his sandwich.

"I guess he's not such a bad old fellow," said Linus. He took a bite of sandwich.

They chewed and thought, chewed and thought for a time.

Then Walter set down his sandwich, opened the refrigerator, and took out a carton of milk. "We simply have to get him to change his mind about the whale. I think our only hope is to help him refocus his vendetta on that cougar."

"Poor cougar." Linus took two glasses out of the cupboard.

"Perhaps we can make him *think* he got the cougar."

"What do you mean?"

"Are there any taxidermists in Kingscross?"

Linus smiled. "Ones that have a stuffed cougar on hand?"

· "That's exactly what I mean."

Linus nodded. This was going to be good.

"Meanwhile," said Walter, "we need to find Cato and tell him that this time, we *may* be on the same page."

No pun intended, thought Linus.

Ophelia pointed to the circle. "There it is."

Aunt Portia's hand flew to her mouth. "And look at all of that equipment! And those books!" She hurried over to the nearest stack sitting on Cato Grubbs's desk. "Oh my! I can't imagine how old some of these volumes are. And look at this strange language that a few of them are written in—I can't even begin to guess what these are!" The circle was forgotten. Ahab was forgotten. Ophelia was forgotten.

Clearly Aunt Portia was the one to consult about obsession.

Ophelia hated to let her aunt in on the secret, but wouldn't a book lover want the enchanted circle to be used on a regular basis? It was their only hope. Life would be so boring otherwise.

"Aunt Portia!" Ophelia snapped her fingers. "Over here. Please concentrate. There's plenty of time for you to examine these books. But we need your help right now. I need to know about obsession. I need to figure out what makes Captain Ahab tick."

Aunt Portia turned toward her niece, her eyes glowing much like Ahab's did when talking about the white whale, only she didn't look like somebody should shoot her with a tranquilizer dart and make haste about it!

"Well, dear, an obsession with something isn't always about the thing itself, it's about what that thing does to a person *inside*. If you can figure out that, then you can figure out someone who's as devoted to his cause as Captain Ahab is. Have you read the book?" She grabbed one of Cato's tomes, held it to her chest, and promptly sat down on the blue couch. She looked up at Ophelia and patted the cushion next to her.

"I just finished it." Ophelia sat.

"Well then, good. How'd you like it?" Her eyes lit up.

"I enjoyed the story parts."

"I felt the same way. But wasn't it worth wading through the other bits to find out the fate of all concerned?"

Ophelia had to think about it. "Other bits" was a bit of an understatement. There seemed to be hundreds of pages of "other bits." "Actually, yes. Yes it was."

"So let's think about this obsession. It's not about the missing leg but about what that leg stands for." *(No pun intended, as Linus would say.)*

"Walking? Easy mobility? Being complete?"

"Bingo! Being complete. But in a masculine sense. Moby Dick makes Captain Ahab feel like less of a man. That whale took away the very bedrock (foundation) of a man like

Captain Ahab's psyche—the belief that he is in control of his own destiny."

"So it isn't just about revenge; it's about victory. It's about telling the whale, the universe, God, and everybody else that Ahab will always prevail."

She nodded. "That Ahab calls his own shots, so to speak."

Ophelia thought for a while. "Then do we need to help him see that he can still control his life? That having a missing leg doesn't make a difference?"

"Why, not at all, dear. You have to get him to see that he never called his own shots to begin with. We are all in the hands of God."

"This is getting complex," said Ophelia. "How are we ever going to work this out? It makes dealing with Quasimodo seem utterly simple."

"I'm sorry I missed him."

"Me too. You would have liked him."

Aunt Portia stood up and moved toward the door. "Of that I have no doubt. He's always pulled on my heartstrings. I'll go start dinner."

"What are we having?"

"It's a red day: Radish salad, strawberries, red peppers, and spaghetti sauce."

Ophelia wished she hadn't asked.

Aunt Portia paused in the doorway. "I'll keep your secret, dear." She held her hand up to her mouth to stifle a cheerful chuckle. "Oh, Auggie will be furious with me if he finds out about the circle!"

Spoken like a true twin.

"Why is that?"

Aunt Portia arched one eyebrow. "Think about it, dearie.

My name's Portia, my brother is Augustus. You are Ophelia, your brother is Linus."

"All Roman names."

"And Cato was a great ...?"

"Roman orator!" Ophelia cried. "We're related to Cato Grubbs?"

Aunt Portia winked and closed the door. As her footsteps retreated down the steps, Ophelia whispered. "Just when I thought things couldn't get any more strange." She knew better than to run after her. Aunt Portia loved a good mystery and like a good mystery novel would only dole out enlightenment a little bit at a time.

sixteen

Reason? What Good Is That When Your Mind Is Made Up?

Captain Ahab began to stir from his nap. You know the way of it—some snorts, the head begins to loll about the shoulders. It's really not a pretty sight, and that's something you might want to remember the next time you begin falling asleep in class.

The trio had talked over their options. It seemed that giving Ahab something to hunt was diametrically opposed (completely opposite) to showing him the error of his ways. But they figured that if one plan didn't work, the other one might. At this point, it seemed best to try everything they could.

The clock was ticking after all. It was now 7 P.M., and only forty hours remained until the circle would open once again. And to be sure, they couldn't count the middle of the night as a productive time. Not a single one of them hated to sleep. No indeed. In fact, they were all destined to be world-class nappers once they entered college, a place famous for its ability to tire out young people who should be full of energy.

They wisely realized that Captain Ahab and the crew back in Book World would be better served if they were rested.

"Right," said Walter. "We'll get moving in the morning. Linus, are you still all right with finding a stuffed cougar?"

"Aye, aye."

"And Ophelia—"

"Yes, yes," she interrupted, not one to give up her status of "being in charge." *Who does Walter think he is, anyway?* "I'm going to take him over to the Bard River Camp for Kids. I think that might be a good way to show Ahab that things do happen that you cannot control and that sometimes accepting it is the best way to defeat it."

Walter shook his head. "I didn't understand a word you just said, but it sounds brilliant."

Captain Ahab snorted his loudest yet.

"We don't have much time," Ophelia said. "As for tonight, let's do what we did with Quasi: watch a movie and eat lots of good snacks. Linus, you run to the video store. I'll be in charge of the food. And Walter, you keep an eye on Ahab until we're ready to start the film." Ophelia grabbed her purse, one of those hippie-type satchels, from atop her desk. "I'll be back in fifteen."

Linus followed her out of the house and turned right as she turned left, mentally crossing his fingers in hopes that Premiere Video had a copy of *Moby-Dick*.

Meanwhile, after making a cup of strong tea for both himself and his ward, Walter stirred Captain Ahab from his nap. He was bored and he had a lot of questions.

"Thank ye, lad. I'm not prone to sleeping in the middle of the day."

"Or at night. At least not lately."

Captain Ahab eyed him with suspicion. "And how do you know such intimate details of my life?"

116

"The book, sir. I've read *Moby-Dick* as well."

"Curse that foul tome!" he roared. "I curse the day it was ever written, this Herman Melville reaching down into my soul and displaying it for all the world to see."

"It's quite a popular book, too. A lot of people know what I know, I'm sorry to tell you."

Ahab shook a fist in the air. "I don't like this arrangement at all, boy. I don't care to be known by people who I don't have the pleasure, or displeasure, of knowing in return." He suddenly became quiet. "As I drifted off to sleep, I was thinking about the entire arrangement. I cannot doubt that what is written on those pages is my life, my very thoughts. That true enough, this Melville character found a way to work himself into my brain. Indeed, I might be forced to realize that he created me, that each thought was formed by this man outside of myself." His voice lowered. "I cannot say I like this possibility. I feel real, lad, as real as you are." He reached out and touched Walter's arm.

"You are," said Walter. "I feel the pressure of your hand. I hear your voice. You *are* as real as I am. And I have to tell you that I don't understand it either. I just know it to be the case."

"But that doesn't give me comfort. How can something not be understood but still be the case?"

"I guess I've seen enough of it to have a little faith—to say that while I don't know how it happens, I do know that it happens … if that even makes sense, sir."

"Not much sense, lad. I do see what you're saying, but I'm not that kind of man."

"Have you finished reading the book yet?"

Ahab shook his head. "No, lad. I don't know if I can bear it."

Walter couldn't blame him. Was it too late to tell him there was hope?

The light in the captain's eyes blazed to life once again. "It doesn't matter then, does it? I'm doomed to hunt the white whale. It is my destiny. And I will carry it out!"

So much for that, thought Walter.

Captain Ahab pointed at the television screen. "Look at that fellow! He looks like a banker. His skin is smooth, and it appears that he hasn't stepped foot on a ship for even a day."

"That's because he hasn't. He's an actor, remember?" Ophelia handed Captain Ahab an oatmeal cream pie. It was his third since the movie began—a three-hour movie, to be exact. She'd explained the characters to him in light of plays and operas. Of course he got it. One thing you can say for Captain Ahab, the man is a quick study (someone who catches on without your having to explain things over and over and over again; the opposite of a dullard).

"You'd think they could find someone more appropriate to play the part."

"Well, we're the only ones who've ever met you, Captain. So how could the filmmakers know?"

He grunted. "The lad playing Starbuck is doing a good job of it. Only Starbuck is not nearly as fine-looking as that fellow."

Ophelia didn't know what the real Starbuck looked like, but she had to agree that the on-screen version was quite good-looking.

The movie wore on and the film version of Captain Ahab got crazier and crazier. Meanwhile, our Captain Ahab kept eating oatmeal cream pies and getting more and more jittery.

Linus sat back and watched. *Is it the sugar or the story?*

When the movie showed Captain Ahab and his harpooneers

entering into a blood brother sort of pact by cutting their hands with the razor-sharp tip of a harpoon (which the sea captain had beat out on the anvil himself), our Captain Ahab actually threw the remainder of his oatmeal cream pie at the screen. "What foolishness is this? Obviously I want nothing to do with the Almighty after what happened to me, but this sort of thing? It seems a silly thing to me. And it certainly did not happen on my *Pequod*!" he roared. "In fact, almost none of this happened, and may I say that Moby Dick is large to be sure, but he isn't that large. Can any living thing be that large? And where did they find a whale that large for this, this—"

"Movie," supplied Walter. "Short for moving picture."

"Aye, this *movie*. And how did they make the beast do the things they wanted it to do? In my experience the great sperm whale cannot, nor should not, be constrained by the wishes of a mankind so small."

Great. I thought we were done with the speeches, thought Linus as Ophelia tried to explain the seemingly magical workings of computer-generated imagery. The concept would have been better explained by Linus. But he figured Captain Ahab was heading back through the portal soon enough, so there was no need for him to understand CGI more thoroughly.

On the screen, the harpooneers, Ishmael, and Captain Ahab clasped their bloody hands. "I just don't understand why they would think such lengths are necessary. What a ridiculous scene!" spat our Captain Ahab.

Ophelia paused. "You want to know why, sir? It's because they had to give the crew a reason not to mutiny."

"Obedience to the captain isn't enough?!" he roared again.

The man loved a good roar, as I'm sure you've noticed by now.

"Not these days," said Walter. "We've become more independent, more suspicious of people in authority. More apt to take matters into our own hands."

"Just like you and the whale," said Linus.

"So whoever wrote the script for this modern-day version of the movie realized that it would be unrealistic, nowadays, for a crew that clearly outnumbers its captain and mostly agrees with the first mate to blindly follow someone who—I hate to say it—has no regard for his crew's well-being," Ophelia said.

What Ophelia just explained was something we call "motivation." Motivation gives the character a good reason for why they do what they do. And sometimes when a character is going to do something extreme, the motivation must be extreme as well. Now whether a blood brothers pact is extreme enough to make a man forget his own life and the lives of others, well you can decide for yourself. I suspect that sometimes the movie industry adds these things for the drama alone. Oh, and the sentimental glurge (words or events that appeal to people's emotions in a way no thinking person shouldn't see right through) they employ time after time makes me want to wipe the sugary residue right off the screen!

Finally, the movie ended. Captain Ahab got up from his seat in the beanbag chair. "So then. That is my fate?"

"It doesn't have to be!" cried Ophelia. "You can change it. Quasimodo did."

"Who's Quasimodo?"

They briefly told him the tale of their last adventure.

"Well, that was the young hunchback," said Captain Ahab. "If I change my fate, it will be only because I won—because

I hunted down Moby Dick and brought him to his death. I know better what to do now."

"And let's face it, the whale isn't that big. I don't know if he could do that amount of damage to the *Pequod*," said Linus.

"Linus!" both Walter and Ophelia shouted.

"But that has nothing to do with you and all the men in the boats," said Walter.

"Aye," said Captain Ahab. "And those are the men who are closer to me, who are more likely to do as I say."

Linus plopped his forehead into his hand. He'd never seen anyone so stubborn in all his life.

But Ophelia saw a look in Captain Ahab's eyes. *Is it defeat?* she wondered. *Certainly it was a look of thoughtfulness. Maybe there was hope. But then again ...*

"I don't seem as crazy as that man, do I?" asked the captain.

The silence of the trio answered with a resounding YES!

Linus offered his bed to Captain Ahab. "Sir, you're the captain."

Captain Ahab offered no argument. By this time, and despite the earlier nap, he was ready to sleep and perhaps escape the dark thoughts that the movie had brought on. Now Ahab knew the ending. Now he could more accurately count the costs. The question was, was Captain Ahab truly insane? Linus had to admit that if he was, then all their plans could mean absolutely nothing.

Ophelia got the sea captain settled in, and Linus padded up the steps to the attic. The ploy worked perfectly. Captain Ahab was more likely to get a good night's sleep, and Ophelia thought her brother had a perfectly sound reason to be upstairs for the night. Not *his* reason, but that was the beauty part of the plan.

He flipped on the desk lamp and reached for the composition book he'd found at the back of one of the supply shelves, filled with handwritten words by, he presumed, Cato Grubbs. He opened it and sat down on Cato's wooden desk chair on wheels—the kind you see in old libraries sometimes. *(Usually seen in the libraries of smaller towns where they don't care if you need ergonomically designed [better for the human body] furniture. There's only so much money, you know.)*

If there were a competition for the world's worst handwriting, Linus would rival every doctor or six-year-old child with undeveloped fine motor skills (the ability to do things like knit, draw, or screw in very small screws with a Phillips head screwdriver). That evening, however, it stood him in good stead because if Linus could read his own handwriting, then he could read Cato Grubbs's scratchings. Much to his delight and perhaps some surprise, Linus realized that Cato's writing looked remarkably like his own. Why hadn't he seen it before? Obviously Aunt Portia had been speaking the truth, and Linus would have been lying if he told you it didn't give him a small thing to know such scientific genius ran through his veins. If Cato could discover how a circle like this worked, surely he could figure out cold fusion someday! (Ask your science teacher. I just work in the English Department. Thank you.)

In the notebook Cato Grubbs, like any scientist worth his salt (someone who lives up to his title)—mad or otherwise—had recorded his experiments in great detail. The elements he used and in what amounts, the length of time between additions, and whatnot. *(I'm no scientist, as you might well guess, and I'm perfectly comfortable with that.)* Cato also recorded what happened and the final results. I, and most likely you, would read such a manuscript and think, *Good heavens, this is* English? However, Linus followed along as though he were born to read such words—which, if you believe at all like I do, he was.

Finally, at 3 A.M. having begun to grasp the principles behind the enchanted circle (which really wasn't "enchanted" at all if you understand the space-time continuum, the magnetic field, and the power of positive thinking), Linus headed to bed and considered it an evening well spent.

seventeen

Good Breakfasts, Bad Boats, and Stuffed Animals Do Not Necessarily Save the Day, but They Sure Beat Duct Tape and a Piece of String

Linus and Ophelia descended on the captain, waking him up and informing him that they had a big day ahead of them.

"Does it include stalking that cat?" he asked.

"We hope so," said Linus.

"It will keep my senses honed for my return to the *Pequod*," he said.

Linus and Ophelia locked eyes. This was going to be harder than they thought.

Aunt Portia entered Linus's bedroom with a fully loaded breakfast tray. Pickled herring, boiled potatoes, sausage, roast beef, and pumpernickel toast. Clearly she wasn't going for a theme that morning. Her curiosity over meeting Captain Ahab had overtaken her normal *modus operandi* (way of doing things), and she was content to dump whatever was at hand on a platter.

"I thought some breakfast might be agreeable," Portia said as she set the tray on Linus's desk. Then she turned to Captain Ahab with an extended hand, "I heard we had a houseguest. I'm Portia Sandwich."

"Captain Ahab, ma'am," Ahab stood, and bowed slightly as he took Portia's hand, his eyes sparkling. And who could blame him? Portia had gone to great lengths with her personal appearance that morning. She'd tamed her usual halo of apricot-colored frizz into a gathering of ringlets at the back of her head, applied a bit of blush and lipstick, and clad her slender body in a simple black dress. No tiara or gauze or tulle or velvet or sparkly items adorned her person.

Ophelia didn't know quite what to make of it, but she kept her mouth shut. Linus didn't notice the difference in his aunt's appearance. He was still pondering last night's chemistry lesson. He would have said physics had a lot to do with it as well. But then physics has something to do with everything, doesn't it? So why bother talking about it?

"Lovely to meet you, Captain. I'm the children's aunt. Now here's a delightful little repast (meal) to break your fast, sir." She removed the plate from the tray and set it on the desk with some cutlery, and then poured him a cup of strong tea from a small silver pot. "Have a seat."

"Ahh, a proper breakfast! Thank you kindly, madam." Captain Ahab sat down with pleasure and began consuming the odd assortment of foods as if it were his usual everyday meal at eight in the morning. *(And it was. Portia knows this manner of information.)*

"So tell me about life aboard the *Pequod*," Aunt Portia asked, sitting next to Ophelia on the bed.

He squinted at her. "So you're knowing who I am and how I got here, then?"

"Of course. It's marvelous, isn't it?" The love of intrigue

danced in Portia's eyes. Ophelia felt a string of dismay wind around her. Would they really have to share the enchanted circle with Aunt Portia? Every time? Honestly, that might not make it as much fun.

The meal progressed as Portia asked Ahab question upon question about life aboard his ship. She sighed in wonder, clapped her hands in excitement, and chortled with laughter when the captain added a humorous quip to his tale, such as that time when one of the crewmembers actually fell inside a whale's head. Obviously he was one of those old people who repeated their stories again and again. "If there was a way to capture a moment in time, madam, I would have used it just to see, over and over, the expression on his face as we pulled him out."

His face changes completely when he's laughing and happy, thought Ophelia.

"Well, we could send you back with a camera," Aunt Portia said.

Ahab squinted at her. "I've been seeing these things called *photographs*. I can take them myself?"

"It's brilliant!" Walter said. "We'll just have to send you back with a lifetime supply of batteries."

Linus knew it wouldn't be so simple. Where would the captain download the picture files? And how would he look at them without electricity? Maybe Linus could figure out how to run a generator off of whale oil and send Ahab back with one of those. His brain began to churn the puzzle round and round.

An hour later, Captain Ahab was washing up in the bathroom. *(As it turned out, Ahab loved being as clean as possible, now that it was so easy to accomplish.)* The trio was waiting on the captain, ready to embark on the day as planned. Linus and Walter were to find the stuffed cougar, and Ophelia was to accompany Captain Ahab to the children's summer camp along the Bard River.

Ophelia remarked to the boys about the captain's changed demeanor with Aunt Portia. "Maybe we've got another element to add to the strategy."

Walter, having completed another round of push-ups, stood,"Well, why not? We might as well confuse ourselves even more. What is it?"

"Joy. I mean, think about it," Ophelia sat on the bean-bag chair. "What must life be like, really, on a whaling ship? Even though he's obsessed with a life at sea, in a way, does he have cause for joy?"

"Maybe years ago he did," said Linus.

"It sure doesn't seem like it now though, does it?" said Walter.

"What about his wife and child?" asked Linus.

"Not even they could make him overcome the obsession that has taken over him. Today we call them workaholics. Maybe the way to work on his obsession is to get him to remember how happy whaling used to make him. And then we need to show him that if he continues with his vendetta against Moby Dick, he'll never be able to sail the seas again— and wouldn't that be a shame?" said Ophelia.

"I like it," said Linus. "You do that."

Ophelia rolled her eyes. "Oh believe me, Linus, I wouldn't begin to leave that sort of thing up to you." She paused. "No offense."

"None taken."

By ten o'clock they'd gone their separate ways. Only twenty-three hours left to convince Captain Ahab to sink his obsession with Moby Dick into the deepest ocean trench.

And that would be the Marianas Trench, by the way, the deepest point on earth. If you didn't know that, then I can safely assume you haven't been listening in geography class. Any second grader should know that fact. Or maybe you have a terrible geography teacher, in which case you should tell your parents so they can complain to the administration. That's what they're there for, after all. "The squeaky wheel gets the grease," so they say, which means that people who complain the loudest for attention will receive it.

Ophelia had called Eric, the young director of the Bard River Camp for Kids, and asked him if she might bring Walter's uncle to the camp. "He's a little eccentric, if you know what I mean," she'd explained on the phone. "He's recently lost a leg, and I thought it would be good for both the kids and Walt's uncle to set their eyes on each other."

Ophelia had first come to know the camp director during last month's flash flood. But since that time, she'd spent hours volunteering at the camp. She even held a children's story hour and craft time twice a week, all having to do with great literature.

Ah, yes, Ophelia's a girl after my own heart.

"Why are we going to—what do you call it, lass—a *summer camp*? And what is a summer camp?" asked Captain Ahab as they crossed the street.

Had I been asked the question, I would have answered that a summer camp is a place where parents—who either don't like having their children around or who think their children are prodigies at music, creative writing, science, or engineering—send their children for a good stretch of time so they don't have to do their job as parents.

However, Ophelia told Ahab *(and I supposed it's from experience)*, "Oh, summer camp is the best! I used to go to Camp Little Falls every year. There were lots of girls there, and we fished—"

"*You* fished?" Ahab raised his eyebrows.

"Uh-huh. And we hiked. And we swam and roamed around the lake in paddleboats—"

"Boats?"

"Yes, sir."

They were strolling by the park now, which was still quiet that summer morning except for the gurgling of the river and the breeze ruffling the leaves on the trees. Ophelia explained the size and way a paddleboat functions, and Ahab waved a hand of disgust.

"It's actually fun, Captain, and nobody pretends it's a *real* boat. Think of it more like going for a canoe ride, only your feet do the work."

He nodded. "All right. That sounds more reasonable—although I might suggest calling it a *paddle-canoe* instead of bestowing it with the title of *boat*."

Good grief, Ophelia thought, *I didn't call it a paddle* ship!

"Do they have these special canoes at this camp?"

"No."

"And why not? Do they think they're too good to get out on the water, lass, is that it?" He was one decibel (a unit of sound intensity) away from a roar.

Ophelia tucked her hand in the crook of his arm. "Not at all. The Bard River can get a little fast, that's all. And they're just kids. So let me tell you about the camp!"

Ophelia explained that the Bard River Camp for Kids, founded back in 1933, was for children with physical disabilities or terminal illnesses. They came to the camp to be with other kids facing challenges like theirs, feel comfortable, and participate in activities designed just for them.

Captain Ahab cocked an eyebrow. *"Physical disabilities, you say? Are those fancy words for what I think you mean?"*

"Yes," Ophelia admitted.

"Well, why would I want to go there?"

Oh great. I opened my mouth too soon, Ophelia thought with a sigh. Then she tried another approach, "Well, why *wouldn't* you?"

"Because I'm not like them, if that's what you're thinking."

"Why would I think that?" Ophelia asked.

"Well, all right then. Just so you're not thinking I need special treatment for what Moby Dick did to me ... that I'm not just as capable a man as I was before the dreaded day dawned, and I was—"

"I wouldn't dream of it, sir," Ophelia gently stopped the captain before he could get on another roll about the white whale. *Oh brother. Some people's pride!* she thought.

As they drew closer to the camp, Captain Ahab quietly studied his surroundings. A collection of dark brown wooden buildings, the camp was spread out on about three acres of land. Mature shade trees stood around the cabins and the lodge. A swimming pool glistened in the sunlight.

As Ahab and Ophelia entered the lodge building at the center of the campgrounds, they were greeted by Kyle, the most outgoing of the children. He'd just done a marvelous 360-degree spin in his wheelchair.

"Ophelia!" he cried and zoomed over to her. His white-blond hair seemed to soak up the sun streaming through the wall of windows overlooking the Bard River, which ran along the edge of the camp.

Ophelia leaned over and embraced the boy as she always did. She loved the warmth of the little boy—and not just from his hugs, but from a heart that was far from disabled. Ophelia often thought that if everyone in the world was like Kyle, then no one would kill another living thing, and we'd all have enough to eat. *(A noble goal of character that we'd all do well to strive to achieve, I might add. Some of us are closer than others, if you know what I mean.)*

The other kids in the lodge left their free-time activities and joined Kyle, Ophelia, and Captain Ahab near the door. Ophelia hugged all of them except Alec who didn't go for that sort of thing but gave her a shy wave instead. She introduced the children to "Uncle Ahab."

"How much free time do you all have left?" she asked.

"Twenty-three minutes," said Kyle.

"Let's play a game!" Ophelia clapped her hands and then turned to Eric, the camp director who always seemed to be a little bit in over his head (that is to say, overwhelmed), and asked, "Is that all right?"

Eric nodded a bit too heartily. "And while you're doing that, I'll go return some phone calls."

Earlier that morning she'd researched some children's games from the 1800s, hoping to zero in on one that Captain Ahab might have played as a child. She figured Ring around the Rosie was as good a place to start as any. If Captain Ahab could remember, even for a second, what it was like to be a kid again, then it would be one step further along the path to success.

Oh, the naiveté of the young!

Linus and Walter entered the Dan the Man's Taxidermy and were immediately—to use the common vernacular (everyday speech) of young people these days—"creeped out." *(I'm sure I don't have to explain the meaning of that expression to you!)*

Walter whistled softly. "Wow."

"Yeah ..." Linus walked over to look a stuffed water buffalo square in the eye.

"Takes a special person to be around this sort of thing all day long, doesn't it?" Walter reached out and tentatively touched the fang of a wolf standing next to the door. "Do you think this is a good idea? I mean, really. Maybe we can just get over to the toy store, buy a large stuffed lion, tie a string to it, and be done with it."

Linus would have readily agreed had the shop owner not just walked out of the back room.

If Jack the shoe repairman looked like a Siberian husky, then Dan the Man looked like a whippet (similar to a greyhound). Long, lean, bright-eyed, and alert, he asked, "Can I help you boys?" His tone was clipped and dried out, much like the animals that surrounded them, yet contained some of the enthusiasm reflected in his eyes.

Walter spoke up, "We were wondering if you have any cougars in your shop?"

Dan the Man stifled a grin. "An unusual request. What is it for?"

"A school project," said Walter.

"In the summertime?"

Blast! Think quick!

"Actually, it's a camp project," offered Linus. "Nature camp."

"Ah. Well, no cougars. I do have a lynx, though." He pointed to a table near the door to the back room, where a smaller cat with hairy ears looked like it was hissing at them.

"Too small," said Linus.

"Do you know of any other taxidermists nearby?" Walter asked.

"There's no one else for a good sixty miles. And the nearest one isn't very good, to be honest. If he had a cougar, it would most likely look like anything but." Dan the Man leaned forward. "His dogs look like cats and his cats look like possums. I don't know how he does it."

Linus raised his brow. He guessed a little professional rivalry was to be expected even among taxidermists.

"Does it have to be realistic?" the taxidermist asked.

"At least from afar," said Linus.

A puzzled expression appeared on Dan the Man's face. "Odd. Well, you might try the toy shop. Some big cat is usually lurking about in there. Now if you'll excuse me, I've got to get back to work. Three dogs died in the past two days and time is limited as you can guess."

They exited the dark shop, and the morning sunlight blasted their retinas. Walter shaded his eyes with the blade of his hand. "Well, that didn't go well."

Linus shrugged. He'd figured it was a long shot, but they had to at least try. "Toy store?"

"Lead the way, mate."

eighteen

Sometimes When You Find Yourself on the Same Side as Some People, You Have to Wonder about Yourself

Captain Ahab wanted to get back on the computer to see the response to his post on a historical site about whaling ships. They made it all sound so difficult, and it was; but men were heartier back then, he thought. They weren't used to electricity and refrigerators and indoor plumbing. All of these hardships were just matter-of-fact. Not that people today *weren't* of a strong constitution; they just took all of their modern-day gadgets and conveniences for granted. These modern fellows made whaling ship crews sound like heroes when they were just doing a day's work for a day's pay.

Except aboard the *Pequod*.

Ahab felt the cold hand of guilt squeeze his heart. They needed to get more whale oil; Starbuck was right. His crew needed to feed their families back home. But all in due time! The ship's hold (the space for carrying cargo) would contain Moby Dick's oil before another whale was caught. And think of how much oil that monster would provide! They'd thank him then. Yes, surely they would. After that, they could go after all of the whales they wanted. He would see that they were handsomely rewarded—even if he had to give up some of his own share of the profits.

Meanwhile, Ophelia received a big surprise when she entered the attic. Cato Grubbs was sitting on the blue couch eating a peanut butter and jelly sandwich. He wore a pair of gray trousers, a violet brocade waistcoat (vest), and a cream-colored shirt with voluminous (full) sleeves and a foam of ruffles at the neck. His curly gray hair, longish and resting on the back of his neck, flowed away from his broad forehead.

"Hello, Ophelia," he said. "Fancy meeting you here."

Ophelia froze. "Where's Starbuck?"

"Oh, heard then? I thought so. That shoe repairman always gets a little too chatty with his customers. Have a seat. I wanted to tell you how nicely things worked out the last time."

"Did you get Esmeralda's emerald necklace?"

"No, thanks to you. Quasimodo made sure to hide it. But at least Frollo got his just desserts. I couldn't stand that man!"

"He did seem rather annoying," she said. "And cruel."

Cato waved a hand, the ruffle on his cuff trailing after the gesture. "Cruel I can deal with. Whining is a greater challenge."

Ophelia hated to agree, but the man was right about that.

"What are you doing here?" she asked, searching his features for any family similarities and finding her mother's nose and Aunt Portia's eyes. Strangely enough, when he squinted he looked like an old, overweight Linus. Much shorter, of course.

"Have you finished reading the book?" He popped the last bite of sandwich into his mouth.

"Yes. It's quite tragic. But that's not surprising considering the time period in which it was written."

He sighed. "Believe it or not, that's why I brought Starbuck back. Even I have a conscience, Ophelia."

She could hardly believe that, but she kept her mouth shut. "There must be something in it for you, Mr. Grubbs."

He laughed, rearranging a ruffle on his shirt. *(My goodness, how many ruffles does one fellow need?)* "Good girl. I thought you were smarter than the average teenager. Of course there is."

"What?"

"In due time … if at all. Now, you do realize we may want the same thing, don't you?"

She crossed her legs beneath her. "Yes. For the sake of the men on the *Pequod.*"

"Exactly."

"But what if Captain Ahab changes while he's here? Can't he go back and make things right?"

Cato stood up. "Young lady, with all due respect, men like Ahab don't change. They never can and they never will. You just have to be a student of human nature. But never you mind. When you've been alive as long as I have, you'll see that we're all stuck in some sort of mold. We can only remake it to very little extent."

"You really believe that? You don't think people can change?" Oh, she clearly hoped that wasn't the case. How awful!

"Oh they *can*. But the question is, *will* they change? And that, dear Ophelia, hardly ever happens. Especially to people like Captain Ahab. You see, he no longer needs a good justification to do what he's doing. He doesn't care. And when people stop caring, that's when they get into real trouble." Cato stood.

Ophelia stood too. "Why did you come here?"

"Because this time I want to make sure you don't foul up my plans!"

"Why not just go into another copy of the book after Captain Ahab goes back?"

"That's not the way it works. Once you open a book in the attic circle, all the other copies become locked, so to speak."

"Is that why what we do is so important to you?"

"Yes."

Ophelia sat back down. This wasn't good news. "So every time we open the circle—"

"You'll have me to deal with. I'm sorry, but that's just the way it is."

"Great. Just great. So where is Starbuck?"

Cato relaxed on the sofa once more. "Back at my house. He's got it all shipshape."

Let me tell you, my dears, and it pains me to do so, when the trio found Quasimodo at Cato's little pink shack in the shabby part of town, the filth would have knocked you over! Months worth of dishes piled up. Dust on every surface dust can land. Horrors I cannot write about without hyperventilating.

"That's a relief," Ophelia muttered.

Cato reddened. "I'm too busy a man for housekeeping. Surely you can understand that. Besides, I've seen your room."

Oh. Now it was Ophelia's turn to blush. "That's neither here nor there. Why didn't you bring him?"

"After dragging Frollo all over Kingscross, I learned it's best not to parade the Book World beings around our world, if you can help it."

"So what's your plan?"

"Well, first off, I told Starbuck the fate of the *Pequod*, which he didn't take too well, you might assume."

Ophelia nodded. "Hey, would you like an oatmeal cream pie?" she asked.

"Yes, thanks."

She handed him the snack and listened as he explained things over the crackle of the cellophane wrapping. It was a good plan, but for everyone's sake aboard the *Pequod*—especially Captain Ahab—Ophelia hoped it wouldn't come to that.

"I find I'm a little fond of that crabby old man," she said to Cato.

"Good for you, Ophelia. If you can like a man like that, then you shouldn't have any problem getting along in the world."

Cato's words sounded nice, but she rather doubted he meant them.

"I'd hate for them to mutiny, Mr. Grubbs. It would be so sad for such a proud man to be humiliated like that."

"That would be the best thing, as I see it." Cato reached for another pie.

"What do you mean?" Ophelia, remembering the awful pink shack, balled up the empty cellophane wrappers and pitched them into the wastebasket.

He leaned forward, a menacing look on his face. "If you can't convince Mr. Starbuck to mutiny, Ophelia, things will get a bit hairy."

"Me? Why me?"

"He already doesn't trust me."

Now that I can believe, thought Ophelia. "And if I can't convince him?"

I'll do my best to make sure Captain Ahab is as far away from the circle as I can get him when the portal opens back up."

"You wouldn't!"

"Oh, I can promise you that. I've seen it happen before and if it happens again, I know I'll survive just fine." His eyes matched the ice in his heart.

Poor Captain Ahab! Ophelia thought. "We'll still try to change him, Mr. Grubbs. We have to. We'll beat you at your own game."

"Have fun trying." He bit down into the cream pie, chewed twice, then swallowed. "I have a feeling that you might not be so quick to use the circle next month. I didn't think you would have the fortitude to try it of your own volition (choosing). Actually I'm rather impressed at your bravery."

"Then why not get rid of the circle?" she asked.

He raised a brow. "I have my reasons and they are none of your business. I'd better get along before that first mate gets cabin fever."

"One more question," said Ophelia. "Why is it so important to you that the Pequod makes it back to Nantucket?"

"Mr. Starbuck is giving me half of his share if we make it home with a full hold and all the crew alive."

"I knew it!" She crossed her arms at her chest and cocked her head. "You're going to buy up as much scrimshaw as possible, aren't you?"

He chuckled and patted her shoulder. "Why, you're a devious one, aren't you?" He walked to the attic door and turned the handle. "But at least you come by it honestly."

He winked at her and left the room.

Ophelia plopped back down on the blue couch. He thought he was leaving her with a mysterious line meant to make the itch of "why did he say that" scratch at her brain.

The joke was clearly on him.

Ophelia smiled.

nineteen

Calling All Boys! Your Delight at Making Good Sound Effects with Your Mouth and Hands May Come in Handy One Day

*W*alter was tired, Linus was hungry, and Walter was tired of hearing about how hungry Linus was.

"Really, mate. I'm not overjoyed about getting off this bus with this blasted lion," Walt growled. Why it was up to *him* to carry the thing, he didn't know. He might have made an issue of it, but figured it wasn't worth it.

This is called choosing carefully which hill to die on. You probably hear people say that a lot. I've found, however, that some people have more hills than any of us can appreciate. Walter was, in short, sacrificing an argument with Linus for more important matters.

Linus fumed; his empty stomach sure wasn't helping matters. But realizing he wasn't about to carry that stuffed lion around town, he remained mute about the situation as well. *(As some of the students at the university say, "Big shocker there!")*

Really, thought Walter thoughtfully petting the lion's mane as the bus lurched back toward the downtown, *this plan has about as much possibility of succeeding as Captain Ahab conquering a whale like Moby Dick. And am I really sitting here petting a toy lion?*

With Captain Ahab composing an online essay back at Seven Hills, hunting and pecking away for the right letters on the keyboard *(you have to give the man credit for his perseverance, if nothing else)*, Ophelia, Walter, and Linus had gathered at Father Lou's manse to set down their plan for the hunt.

Father Lou gathered his long white hair into a ponytail and then pointed at the stuffed lion. "Really? You think that's going to fool him?"

Linus bristled. "Do we have another choice?"

Walter followed suit. "After all the trouble it took to get this blighter (that's British slang for "rascal"), it had better work!"

Ophelia shook her head with a grunt. "At least you didn't have to deal with a grumpy old man at the kids' camp. What a curmudgeon (bad-tempered person)! After one round of Ring around the Rosie, I knew I had to get him out of there. He simply wouldn't fall down. In fact, he refused. He just jutted out that beard of his, crossed his arms, and stalked out of the room."

Father Lou laughed. The three teens didn't regret letting the priest of All Souls in on the secret of the enchanted circle. In his younger days, Father Lou had made his living as a bounty hunter—someone who goes after people with arrest warrants on their heads, finds them, sometimes fights them, and then brings them in to the authorities. And for their efforts, they get paid a bounty (reward). Some bounties are larger than others, according to how dangerous a criminal might be. *(You see? Some remnants from the Old West are still alive and well to this very day! It warms my heart.)*

Father Lou arose from his seat at the kitchen table to fetch the teapot. "And what is the point of having Captain Ahab hunt down a stuffed toy from the mall?"

He made the plan sound even crazier than it was. At least Ophelia thought so. But she was ready to try anything. The thought of Captain Ahab painfully fizzing in the acids between Book World and Real Word was nothing short of horrific. Who wanted to see that? No. They had to try their best. Anything less than that simply wouldn't do.

"Here's the thought behind the plan, Father Lou." Ophelia reached across the table for a slice of coffee cake, the kind with delicious cinnamon crumbles on top. *(Oh joy! Couldn't you eat a piece of that right now? I know I could. Please don't get crumbs everywhere. Thank you.)*

"We're hoping that if he gets the cougar, or at least *thinks* he does, it will satisfy his vendetta."

Father Lou leaned forward. "Go on."

"And then—" she shifted in her chair.

"This whole thing sounds ridiculous now that we're telling it to an adult," interrupted Walter.

Linus blew out a puff of air as he nodded his agreement.

Ophelia started over. "And *then* there's another thing. We're hoping that when Ahab sees that the 'dead cat' was never real to begin with, he'll realize that his elation at hunting it was never about the true outcome; it was about the thrill of the chase. That in the end, it didn't really matter at all."

"Well, good job on the psychology of all that, Ophelia," said Father Lou as he stirred the leaves in the pot and set a small strainer over the first teacup he had lined up on the counter. A line of three teacups, to be exact. Linus had finally come clean that he wasn't all that fond of the stuff. "But I gotta wonder if Ahab will react that way. You never know, though. Isn't that right?"

Oh, great, thought Linus. *This is going to be a disaster.*

"The most you can do is try. But what will you do if he's still bent on hunting down Moby Dick?"

Walter took the teacup that Father Lou held out to him. "We don't know. We'll most likely have a moral dilemma on our hands."

The priest scratched his cheek. "Whether to send him back to wreak havoc on his crew or let him melt away—that is the question."

"Sacrifice the one for the many." Walter spooned sugar in his tea.

"To be or not to be, when you get right down to it," said Ophelia.

Father Lou smiled. "Exactly." He sat back down and cut a piece of coffee cake for himself. "Well, I don't have a better plan."

"Will you help us, then?" asked Walter.

"Sure! I've been down in the basement all month, trying to fix the damage from the flood. If I have to go through another soggy cardboard box just to see if there's anything worth saving inside, I'll explode. Let's lay down a game plan and just see what happens … although I'm not overly optimistic, I'm sorry to say."

"We do have a backup plan. Sort of." Ophelia stabbed her slice of coffee cake with her fork.

"What do you mean?" asked Walter.

"You're not going to believe this." She then filled them in on Cato's visit to the attic and his plans.

"Brilliant!" said Walter. "And you're sure Starbuck will comply if we can't get Captain Ahab to change?"

"It's up to me to convince him. Cato said Starbuck doesn't trust him."

Linus barked out a laugh.

Father Lou set a piece of paper on the table. "I think the best place for this to happen is in the woods along the Bard River, up at Joan Dawson's soybean farm near the old dam." *(Joan was surprisingly well read and came into the bookshop at least once a week.)*

"Perfect," said Ophelia.

They drew up a map and then decided the right time of day and who would do what.

"We're doomed," said Walter. "This is ridiculous."

Father Lou patted him on the back. "I don't know, Walt. Sometimes we have to have a little faith. There have been crazier successes in the course of human history than this. And we've got this to help us." He cupped his hands to his mouth and made the loudest cat roar they'd ever heard.

"Oh my!" Ophelia jumped in her chair. "Now *that* is something we can work with. Maybe we'll succeed after all."

twenty

If You're Going to Hold a Mutiny, You'd Better Have a Better Reason Than "It Seemed Like a Good Idea at the Time"

*W*hat Cato wasn't telling the children was that he'd had plenty of mishaps during the first stages of experimentation. Back in those days, he couldn't focus the portal on just one *copy* of the book. No sir! He zeroed in on the final story itself.

Have you ever read *The Importance of Being Duplicitous*? Of course not. And you never will either, what with it being wiped from the face of literature for all eternity—past, present, and future. And how about *The Untamable Shrew*?

I thought so.

He was worried the circle might malfunction one day, but like any good scientist, he wanted to see what happened if it did.

Figuring it was better not to risk Uncle Augustus discovering the current happenings, Ophelia suggested instead that she and Starbuck talk in Paris Park. Walter accompanied her just in case things got ugly, as they say, and Ophelia needed his help. Linus agreed to stay back at the house and keep an eye on Captain Ahab during a viewing of *Mutiny on the Bounty*.

"Food for thought," he said.

Walter and Ophelia were sitting at a picnic table in a pavilion near the Bard River when Cato and Starbuck approached.

"Oh, I love that old river," Cato said, grunting a little as he climbed over the bench and slid his legs underneath the tabletop. He nodded at Ophelia. "Well, Mr. Starbuck, Ophelia here is well aware of your plight aboard the *Pequod*." Now Cato gestured toward Starbuck. "And Mr. Starbuck is aware of the circle and all that entails, although it wasn't easy to convince him." He turned to Starbuck. "You're not a man of fancy, are you?"

"No, sir." Starbuck had an air about him that was serious but kind.

"He's a practical man," said Cato.

Walter eyed Cato as if to warn him not to try any funny business.

"So go ahead, Ophelia, tell Mr. Starbuck the plan," Cato prodded.

Ophelia laced her fingers together and placed her clasped hands in front of her on the table. This was serious business, and Ophelia knew how to be sober (serious). "Mr. Starbuck, Mr. Grubbs told me that you're aware of the fate of the *Pequod*."

"Yes." He nodded.

Ophelia admired the man right away. All business, yes, but his gaze was open. He didn't seem to have any other agenda than doing the right thing. She liked that.

"Do you think you can get the crew to mutiny?"

He started, sitting up even straighter. "Mutiny? Why, miss, do you understand how serious it is to lead a mutiny?"

"I can't say that I do, but I'd appreciate it greatly if you'd enlighten me." She was wise enough to know that if she knew what the plan would cost him, it might help her to convince him that their plan might be the only way to save lives.

Let me describe Mr. Starbuck for you. He was of a lanky build with a great head of warm brown hair. His austere (without decoration) clothing in dark tones provided a complete visual contrast to that of the overweight and terribly overdressed Cato Grubbs.

Ophelia appreciated Mr. Starbuck's earnest face as he explained, "Sailing on a whaling ship is my life, miss. For most of the crew, I could say the same. For us to mutiny without cause—or what might be perceived as having no just cause by the owners of the *Pequod*—we'll lose our livelihood. We'll lose the respect of all those who we live with in and around Nantucket. In short, life as we know it will cease." He looked down and balled up his hands into fists. "Take a whaling man from the sea, miss, and you might just as well take his life." He looked up, a sadness at the thought deeply imbedded in his brown eyes. Ophelia had to squeeze her eyes shut in order not to tear up.

"It's hard for us to understand that kind of dedication," said Walter.

"It's a *way*," said Ophelia. "It's more than just devotion to something; it's who they are."

"Aye, miss," said Starbuck.

"What was Captain Ahab like? Before Moby Dick took his leg?" she asked.

"A fine captain to sail with. He knew what to do, how to do it, how to bring as much oil back as possible. He was fearless with his harpoon. He's never been a gentle soul, miss, but he treated the crew fairly enough, and he never asked anyone to do what he wasn't willing to do himself. Or at least had done, many times."

"He started as a cabin boy?" asked Walter.

"As did a lot of us."

They all relaxed their spines a bit as two mothers pushing toddlers in strollers walked by, chatting and laughing.

"What about your families?" asked Ophelia, nodding her head in the direction of the ladies and their offspring. "What about all of those men who are fathers? They'd be leaving their wives to raise the children alone. Isn't mutiny worth that? Even if you are implicated of having done it without cause?"

"A man is nothing without honor, miss. Not only I, but the entire crew would be anathema."

It's a biblical word, anathema. *Starbuck, being the good Quaker he was, didn't shy away from such terms. Simply put,* anathema *means something or someone that is particularly loathed and therefore, in this case, most likely kicked onto the fringe of society.*

"Then we have to be sure there's an ironclad reason for you to take over the ship, Mr. Starbuck. Anybody have any ideas?" Ophelia asked.

And so they put their heads together. They were all bright people, canny and practical. And make no mistake, if any group could come up with a solution, it would be those four sitting at a picnic table while the Bard River rolled by, continuing on a course set for it long ago.

twenty-one

You Cannot Always Rely on Someone's Inability to See in the Dark

Twilight approached, that purple-hued time of day when it seems like anything could happen. A light rain had fallen an hour before, and the smell of the woods ahead of them, earthy and fresh, gave Ophelia a bit of optimism. *This really could work, couldn't it? Surely Mr. Starbuck wouldn't have to risk all that he held dear*, she thought.

Father Lou and Walter had gone ahead out in the woods and planted the stuffed lion, which was tied to a strong piece of fishing line. Linus, Ophelia, and Captain Ahab—who was clearly not in the mood to be genial (friendly, cheerful)—set out fifteen minutes after they left. They only had about a ten-minute window in which it would be too dark to get more than a glimpse of the lion, but light enough where it could be seen just enough not to look like something from a children's movie.

This is going to take some delicate timing, thought Linus.

"I do hope we get the timing right," whispered Ophelia.

Captain Ahab walked behind them, muttering to himself.

"And he's beginning to talk to himself," Ophelia continued softly. "That can't be good."

Hardly. Linus didn't have a good feeling about this. They had about fifteen hours to change a man like Captain Ahab. *Good luck with that.*

"You all right back there, Captain?" Linus called over his shoulder.

"Aye, lad! Just lead the way and we'll be rid of that wild cat soon enough. And then rabbits, children, pets, and all other manner of living thing will be all the safer for it. I remember in my early days, as a young lad at sea ... "

"He's giving speeches again," whispered Ophelia.

"Not a good sign," said Linus.

They'd walked almost half a mile by this time, up Bard River Road toward Joan's farm. A belt of woodland hid her soybean fields from the river. "Do you think Father Lou and Walter made it to the dam?" Ophelia murmured.

"Yep."

"I think it will go well, don't you?"

Linus had no doubt the plan itself would play out just fine; but whether or not it would work to turn around someone as determined as Captain Ahab, well, he had plenty of doubts about that!

Certainly, I don't blame him. I think I would have taken my chances and let the old man fizzle away. Good thing I'm not privy to the wonders of the enchanted circle. To whom much is given, much is required, as the Good Book says.

As the sky turned to amethyst, Ophelia and Linus helped Captain Ahab climb over a fence by the road and onto Farmer Joan's property. He did surprisingly well for an old man with one good leg. *(Give credit where credit is due, I always say.)*

"How exactly will you track this thing, Captain? Don't you hunt on the open sea?" asked Ophelia.

He tapped the side of his temple, then tapped his chest over his heart, and then tapped his stomach. "Instinct, my dear. Instinct comes when you know how to listen to all three at once."

Wow, thought Linus, *I like it*.

"Well, then—" Ophelia swept a hand toward the path as they entered the woods. "Go for it."

"Go for it?" Captain Ahab screwed up his face.

"Have at it," said Linus.

"Have at it?" he asked. "Speak the King's English, young ones, so I might better understand you."

"There's no better time than the present!" cried Ophelia.

He stepped onto the dirt path. "You children are the oddest creatures sometimes. But be that as it may, let's begin the hunt, shall we?"

"Now why didn't I just say that?" muttered Ophelia to Linus as they got behind the captain.

Captain Ahab slowed his pace and walked as quietly as he could. He held up a finger to get the direction of the light breeze blowing through the trees. Then he sniffed in the direction from which it came.

He barely shrugged and then proceeded forward. "Here, boy," he said as he reached behind him. "Hand me that gun."

Linus obeyed, but not without a rather desperate prayer that Captain Ahab wouldn't shoot out someone's eye during the hunt.

"It's just a BB gun," whispered Ophelia. "Don't worry."

Suddenly Linus began to wonder if he was projecting messages into Ophelia's mind, or if Ophelia was just picking up his thoughts. Maybe *she* was the one with ESP, not him! Clearly he'd have to experiment with it to make sure.

It was quite impressive how quietly Captain Ahab could walk across the arboreal floor (the ground of the woods). Even when stepping with his prosthetic leg, he barely made a sound. Ahab walked for about fifty yards, then turned. "I see nothing that looks as if the cat has passed this way."

Oh no, he really knows how to track animals! Ophelia thought, then said, "I'm sure it's very different from hunting something at sea. Perhaps you don't know what to look for?" She crossed her fingers in hope.

"Lass, I grew up hunting on land. Where I'm from, you have to hunt if you want to eat. We can't just go to the 'grocery store,' as you call it."

Oh. Where are you guys? she thought desperately. *He needs to see that lion, and quick!*

A loud cat roar bounced off the leaves overhead and filled their ears. Captain Ahab's face lit up, and he held one finger to his lips. They lowered their stance as they tiptoed behind him.

Suddenly a golden cat rump was seen by all! Ahab lifted the gun to his shoulder and shot. Another roar sounded, and the stuffed lion began to move quickly and out of sight.

Father Lou and Walter had realized ahead of time that they'd have to keep just ahead of Captain Ahab's view because, really, there wasn't any way they'd be able to keep that stuffed lion on its feet.

Another roar resounded and for the only time, then or now, the twins were thankful Moby Dick had bitten off the leg of Captain Ahab.

Walter reeled in the beast, grabbed it around the middle, and took off along the path toward the dam. Father Lou was right behind him.

"All right. Let's stand him up at the edge of the river," said Father Lou, a little out of breath.

Walter the Push-Up King looked as if he'd just finished relaxing on a deck with a fruit juice. "Right." He set up the lion, its rear pointed toward the ensuing group, and hoped it wouldn't look quite so fake that way.

Father Lou roared again.

Yes, this really was a stretch. They knew it then; we know it now. But the important thing was to try. Sometimes a far-fetched idea is better than no idea at all. Sometimes it's the reverse. It's all a gamble, really, so don't listen to a word I'm saying. I don't wish to be responsible for any attempt you might make to do something in the future. (My lawyer told me to say that, and for once I agree with him.)

They slid down the embankment and crouched low. Father Lou held the fishing line in his hand to make for a quick pull when the time came.

"Here they come," whispered Walter at the sound of leafy branches being shoved aside.

"Shhh." Father Lou wound the fishing line around his hand and then let out another loud roar.

Walter started. Some sounds one never gets used to.

A few sticks snapped under the feet of the approaching hunting party.

"There it is!" Ahab whispered with excitement and raised the BB gun once more. He took aim and placed his forefinger on the trigger.

"Ow!" Ophelia cried out as a sharp stick penetrated the sole of her flip-flop and the bottom of her foot.

Ahab, startled, pulled the trigger just as Walter rose up at the sound of his good friend's cry.

twenty-two

Over and Under and What Might Be Referred to as Basket Weaving!

*W*alter felt the BB hit his chest, and while it wasn't enough to do any real damage, it caused him to lose his footing and tumble down the riverbank.

"Walt!" Ophelia screamed and started running toward him.

Father Lou pulled the fishing line, and the toy lion fell onto its side and scraped over the edge of the embankment.

"What the devil is going on?" Captain Ahab roared.

"He's fallen into the river!" Father Lou cried as Ophelia, Linus, and the captain hurried up.

Walter knew he was in trouble. He'd never learned to swim, you see. When would he have while scrapping about the streets of a big city like London? Panic overtook him. The water was deep and running fast; and the more he floundered, the further from the bank he got.

"Help!" Walter cried. "Help!" he cried out again as the river, in just a matter of seconds, took him to the center of the dam—the spot that had crumbled during the rains in June. The river was rushing like a small waterfall.

Father Lou had just hardened his leg muscles to push off

the ground and jump in, when Captain Ahab, false leg and all, sprung off the top of the bank, over the priest's head, and into the river.

Let me point out that Ahab didn't think twice about how deep the river was. *That* was who Captain Ahab could be and who he was when as a younger man—before he'd become jaded and before he'd seen so many lives lost. Walter reminded Ahab of his own son, and his fatherly instinct overtook all else.

Ahab sliced into the water cleanly and swam with an easy stroke toward Walter. Ophelia gasped as the two of them went over the dam.

Linus grinned. *What a guy!*

Father Lou climbed into the river and swam in their direction, but catching up to Captain Ahab and Walter wasn't easy. The river had taken them in her arms. Lou said a silent prayer and held his nose as he went over the dam and into the pool below.

Start to drown and you'll never be the same again. Walter had thought he was so tough, and by most standards it proved true. But when a lad is up against the forces of nature, it doesn't matter if he can land a punch right where he wants it to go or beat anybody he knows in an arm wrestling match.

"Hold on, boy! I'm coming for you!"

Captain Ahab?

As Walter went under for a third time, a pair of strong arms hooked under his and began pulling him toward the riverbank where Linus and Ophelia, having run downriver, were now waiting. Relief spread over their faces like the rising sun over the green fields.

Captain Ahab was a strong swimmer. You had to be if you were in the whaling business. Sometimes your harpoon boat was destroyed by one of the leviathans, and you had no choice but to swim to the closest vessel. And that wasn't necessarily as close as you'd like it to be.

Soon enough, Captain Ahab felt the river bottom. "Just stand now, lad. You'll find the good earth beneath your feet."

Walter did as he was told, his legs shaking and his insides quaking from the adrenaline coursing through his veins. Captain Ahab pushed him up as Linus grabbed Walter's arms and pulled. Walter, in one swift move, soon found himself lying on the grass.

"Wow," said Father Lou, swimming up to the bank. "That was scary."

He helped Captain Ahab, who had lost his prosthesis, climb out of the river.

"That was something, Captain," he said. "You saved Walter's life, you know. Impressive. I haven't seen swimming like that since, well, never really—other than during the Olympics, which you probably don't even know about ..." Clearly his nerves were getting the better of him.

As Father Lou continued to chatter like a parrot, Ophelia helped Captain Ahab sit down, and the three river racers lay there catching their breath and letting the reality of what had just occurred sink in. They all shook with post-excitement jitters. It's that feeling you get when your mother or father almost—almost, I say—crash the car.

Finally, Captain Ahab spoke, "I haven't felt that terrible thrill in quite a while!"

This is the strangest man I have ever met, thought Linus.

But Father Lou, having been in more fights and more

close calls than one human being should ever experience, knew exactly what Ahab meant. The thrill of fear. There was nothing else like it.

Oh, you don't understand? Well then, why are roller coasters so popular?

There, I knew you'd get it.

twenty-three

Of Course He Wouldn't Make It Easy on Them! What Were You Even Thinking?

*L*ooking as weary as they'd ever seen him, (and who wouldn't be walking half a mile leaning on two people as if they were crutches?) Captain Ahab bathed and then changed into the clothing in which he arrived, cleaned and pressed, thanks to dear Aunt Portia. Walter was still a bit dazed after having almost met his Maker, and Ophelia and Linus were just plain ready for bed. What a day it had been! And now only thirteen hours remained until the portal opened for Ahab's return journey.

In contrast to staying up all night and eating junk food, playing board games, and watching movies—as they'd done with Quasi before his return through the circle—they all decided the best thing to do was get a good night's sleep. Captain Ahab wasn't the kind of individual three fourteen year olds wanted to pull an all-nighter with anyway.

After making sure their guest's bed was ready and then fetching him a glass of warm milk and a couple of brownies, Ophelia walked toward the attic door.

She turned. "Have a good sleep, Captain Ahab."

He nodded with a grunt, a troubled look on his face.

"Are you going to be all right, Captain?"

"I have much to think about, lass. Today made me see some matters a bit more clearly, that they did."

Is there hope then? Ophelia prayed it was so!

"If you need anything, you know where my room is. Even if it's in the middle of the night, you have only to wake me up."

"Thank you. Good night then, lass."

Ophelia, having decided that she wanted a brownie too, was standing in the kitchen feeling sad. She didn't mind feeling sad; in fact, it made her feel closer to Captain Ahab to try to put herself in his shoes ... uh, shoe.

When she heard a light tapping on the back door of the bookshop, she walked down the steps, looked through the paned glass, and swung the door open.

Goodness! Aunt Portia had forgotten to lock the door again! It's a wonder they were all still alive and had their computers and television set. For truthfully, who can live without those two apparatuses shining in the dark and cluttering up the mind?

"Mr. Starbuck! Come on in!"

The first mate of the *Pequod* took off his cap and stepped through the door. "Good evening, miss."

"Do I have some things to tell you!" she said. "Would you care for a bite to eat? Something sweet? My aunt made brownies this afternoon."

"Thank you, no, miss."

"Then let's just talk." She didn't want to risk having her aunt and uncle see her with another strange man. "Let's go in the backyard. It's a nice evening."

They sat at the picnic table on the patio. The moon was high and lit the backyard enough that the two could see each other's expressions quite easily.

And with the way his lips were pursed, Starbuck was clearly worried.

"Tell me, what concerns you?" Ophelia asked.

"We have to make sure Captain Ahab gets back in that circle, miss. You see, if he disappears, it's well known that I haven't been happy with his orders as of late. The crew will suspect me, most certainly."

"Oh! I hadn't thought of that!"

"Yes, miss. I think it would be better for all of us to just take our chances with the captain as he is—and most likely will continue to be. Now that I know what happens, maybe I can work harder to turn things around."

"Without a mutiny?"

He nodded. "Mutiny will be the last resort."

"He seems to have a way of gathering the sailors into his plans, doesn't he?"

"He's not been a captain all these years because he can't handle a crew."

"Are they afraid of him?"

"Some are. Some aren't. They have different reasons for following his lead."

"What about Ishmael?" she asked.

Ishmael, a first-time sailor on the Pequod, *was the narrator of* Moby-Dick, *much like I'm the narrator of the book you're reading right now. He tells the story.*

"He's not important. He does as good a job as a new sailor can. Queequeg shows him what to do."

"Well, it shouldn't be difficult to get Captain Ahab back

into the circle, Mr. Starbuck. It's what he wants to do anyway. At least I think so."

She related to him the events of the afternoon.

"Did he say he was ready to get back on the ship?" asked Starbuck.

"No. But not long before he retired for the evening, he did say to me that he was ready to do the right thing."

Starbuck relaxed his spine a little. "Good. Good. Then all will be well."

"You and Cato Grubbs should come by just to make sure," she invited. "The circle opens at 11:11 A.M. tomorrow."

Mr. Starbuck placed his cap back atop his head. "We'll be there."

"Mr. Starbuck? Cato stole the captain's ivory leg. He's going to need it."

"I'll hurry back and bring it right over."

"I'll wait here," she promised.

As Ophelia bade him good-bye, she had to admit she wasn't quite as optimistic as Mr. Starbuck. Who could really know what goes on inside the mind of a man like Captain Ahab?

Fifteen minutes later the first mate returned with the leg, bowed stiffly, and made his way back to the pink shack.

And so the night seeped into the cracks and crevices of the town of Kingscross as the trio slept, blissfully unaware that Captain Ahab awoke around 5 A.M., strapped on his old ivory peg-leg, and left Seven Hills Better Books, with BB gun in hand.

You can imagine the horror that Ophelia, Linus, and Walter felt when they brought the sea captain's breakfast to him at eight the next morning—just three hours 'til liftoff—only to find the attic deserted.

"Where could he have gone?" cried Ophelia.

"Dunno," said Walter, still bleary-eyed. He didn't sleep very well after yesterday's scare, and who can blame him?

Linus walked over to the worktable and scraped off a note. "Let's find out." He handed the letter to Ophelia who read it aloud:

> *Dear Children and Mr. Starbuck,*
>
> *Rescuing Walter yesterday gave me quite a lot to ponder, and I've come to the conclusion that my presence on the* Pequod *will only be a detriment to my officers and the crew. I do not trust myself, once back aboard, to do anything other than reignite my passion for hunting and killing Moby Dick.*
>
> *I'll take my chances with the "acids between the worlds"—as you call what happens when one fails to make it through the circle in the attic. It's the best I can do for my men.*
>
> *Please let Mr. Starbuck know. I have left a note for him to find in my cabin after he returns, a note explaining why I took my own life by disappearing into the depths of the sea I've loved all my life.*
>
> *Sincerely yours,*
>
> *Ahab, CAPT.*

"Where do you think he went?" asked Walter, his eyes now wide as he realized just how much he'd come to care about the old sea captain.

"Let's think about this." Ophelia sat down on the blue couch. "Where would a sea captain want to die?"

"He just told us. In the water,," said Linus, finding the second letter and placing it in his back pocket.

"Right." Walter rubbed the sleep completely out of his eyes. "We have to get to the Bard. He'll have quite a jump on us."

"Which direction do you think he went?" asked Ophelia.

The boys shook their heads and shrugged.

"Let's think how we're going to do this while we grab some cereal." Ophelia stood up and headed down to the kitchen.

Father Lou had already disassembled what looked like half of his Harley motorcycle on the parking pad next to the manse. He eyed the trio as they hurried up to him. "I can't wait to hear this," he said.

"Okay." Ophelia nominated herself as the spokesperson. "Captain Ahab has disappeared." She handed him the letter.

The priest set down his wrench and looked at his watch. "Not much time left, is there?" He read the words of Captain Ahab. "Wow."

Ophelia continued, "We figure he'll want to die by the water, and the Bard is it. We have no idea how far he's gone because we have no clue what time he left. Sometime during the middle of the night, though."

"And you need my help, naturally."

"Yes. Walter and I are going to head west along the river, Linus is going east. Can you drive near Linus and bring the captain back with you—if you find him first?" She held up a cell phone. "I borrowed my aunt's cell. If we find him, I'll call you and you can come get him wherever we are."

Father Lou wiped his greasy hands on a rag. "All right. I'll do it. I can't have his disintegration on my conscience—even if he is just a figment of Herman Melville's imagination." Even as Father Lou said it, he knew what the trio was thinking. Captain Ahab was as real as anyone they'd ever known.

Walter felt like walking alongside that river about as much as you would if you'd almost drowned in it the day before. But Ophelia figured, and rightly so, that it was best for Walter to face his fear and walk right beside that dam on Farmer Joan's farm.

"Right," he said, convincing himself as they stopped at the dam. "That was the closest call I've had yet, and I've had some close calls."

"I'm so sorry, Walter. If I'd never cried out, the whole thing wouldn't have happened."

"You couldn't help it. How's your foot, by the way?"

Ophelia winced. "I've got a nice-sized hole in the arch. Of course, I didn't feel it until I got home. It's funny how adrenaline will do that to you."

"Does it hurt to walk?"

"A little."

They looked at the ruptured dam. Ophelia sighed. "We'd best keep going."

"I won't argue with you," Walter said.

Ophelia checked the time on Portia's cell phone: 9:30 A.M.

"I hope we find him soon," she said, more to herself than to her companion.

"I do as well."

Another mile ribboned its way beneath their feet, and neither one had much to say. They'd all agreed to call off the river search at 10:15 A.M. and hunt around Kingscross for a time.

"I don't have a good feeling about this," Ophelia said.

"Me neither. But what else can we do?"

Ophelia shrugged. "I can't believe I'm about to say this. I'm going to miss him."

Walter agreed.

Of course, Father Lou and Linus felt much the same way. As he slowly drove along the Bard, Father Lou listened to the news on the local radio station, hoping to hear some report of a delusional old man being sighted around town. Linus kept hope alive by willing Captain Ahab to appear in his path.

It wasn't much of a hope, really. It was one thing to connect mind-to-mind with his sister, but making something happen by sheer willpower—especially something concerning Captain Ahab—was quite another.

Finally, checking his watch, Linus turned toward the road where Father Lou was waiting.

"It's 10:10," he said.

"Let's get back." Father Lou leaned across the front seat and pushed open the passenger door. "We'll have to think of something else. Let's go get the others."

twenty-four

No Matter How Many People Say It's an Opportunity, Failure Always Feels Like, Well, Failure

Thank goodness Kingscross isn't a large metropolis. Far from it. If you want to find an unusual type of sausage, forget it. Don't even bother to look. A spare part to a 1962 Frigidaire? Well, maybe, but don't expect to find a new refrigerator made to look like a 1962 Frigidaire. You're better off checking the Internet or the big city forty miles away. On the up side, the search party was able to drive up and down every street and visit every fountain—even the city pond near the courthouse. But no watery place yielded Captain Ahab.

"That is one brave man," said Father Lou as he pulled his car back into his driveway.

"I know." Ophelia didn't know if she'd be quite that brave. But Captain Ahab clearly wasn't lacking in courage. Herman Melville had made sure of that.

10:55 A.M.

Sixteen minutes.

"Should we get back to the circle?" she asked the group as they disembarked from Father Lou's old sedan. "I mean, maybe if we put the book in there, something will happen and he'll be whisked back anyway."

Linus didn't want to be the naysayer, so instead he said, "It couldn't hurt."

"All right. Although, no plan of ours has worked out yet." Ophelia sighed and turned, heading back toward the bookshop.

Walter turned to Father Lou. "Mind if I stay here with you and learn about motorcycles?"

"Not at all. What about you, Linus?"

"I shouldn't leave my sister right now." Linus shoved his hands in his pockets and followed after Ophelia. "See you later."

The twins, glum (sad, gloomy, discouraged) beyond all telling, decided to wait in the attic. Cato and Starbuck would be arriving any minute, and they might as well get the news firsthand.

"Do you still have that letter for Starbuck?" she asked.

Linus nodded and patted his back pocket.

"Maybe bringing people over to our world isn't such a good idea after all," said Ophelia, running her hand along the bookcase. "He wasn't so bad."

"I liked him," said Linus picking up a jar of red powder and wondering if he could ask Cato Grubbs to take on a protégé.

"This is too sad," said Ophelia. She plopped down onto the couch and began rhythmically thumping her head against the back of it with her eyes squeezed shut.

At 11:05 A.M., Cato and Mr. Starbuck entered the attic.

"How do you get in here without anyone noticing?" asked Ophelia.

"Secret passage."

"From the school?" asked Linus.

Cato shook his head.

"Captain Ahab? Where is he?" the scientist asked.

"He ran off this morning. Left us a note saying he didn't trust himself anymore. He didn't want the *Pequod* to meet the fate described in the book. He said he'd take his chances with disintegrating."

Starbuck's face lost all color.

"Don't worry," said Linus, handing him the note.

Starbuck unfolded the paper, and his eyes quickly darted through the words written in Ahab's old-fashioned script. *(Don't get me started on what's happened to the state of handwriting these days!)*

He looked up. "It's a suicide note."

"We know. So then everything will be all right for you?" asked Ophelia.

Starbuck cleared his throat. "Captain Ahab and I have sailed together many a year, miss. When he went mad, I felt like I lost a good friend and made an enemy I'd never bargained for."

"But still you obeyed his orders," Ophelia said.

"Aye. But now, seeing this, I feel as if I've lost him all over again, and this time it's for good."

Linus turned to Cato. "Will Mr. Starbuck head back through the portal when it opens?"

"He can." Cato spoke to Ophelia now, "Where will you put him back in, then?"

"The night before the second day of the final hunt. At that point Captain Ahab could ostensibly (seem to) do what he claims to have done in the note to Starbuck. Did he say anything about Moby Dick in the note, Mr. Starbuck?"

"Yes. He said he realized the whale was a devil indeed, and no one wins against the Devil."

11:09 A.M.

Ophelia felt sick to her stomach. This was one of the worst moments of her life. Poor Captain Ahab!

What have we done? thought Linus. The reality of their new friend's demise pushed away all thoughts of experimenting along the same path that Cato had trod. Some things were never meant to be done, he figured. Maybe he wasn't cut out to be a fearless scientist after all.

Suddenly, the attic door swung open and slammed loudly against the wall behind it.

There stood Captain Ahab. He grinned and that crazed glint was back in his eyes.

twenty-five

Never Forget That Sometimes the Sum of All Your Failed Plans Might Equal Something Brilliant— But Not Always

"I knew I'd find that cat if I persevered. And certain enough, there we were, face-to-face on the river path." Captain Ahab tossed the BB gun to Linus. "I think I frightened that critter away for good! And I didn't even need to fire a shot. I just roared at him."

Ophelia jumped to her feet. "Captain Ahab!" She threw her arms around him, got a quick squeeze in return and then a slight push back to where she'd started.

"Thank you, lass."

"What made you change your mind?"

"I have a wife and son that love me, and so do most of my crew. Sudden I saw how important that was." He turned to the rest of the room's occupants. "Now, let's get back aboard the *Pequod*!" he shouted. "We've got a whale to kill!"

Starbuck blanched again.

Oh no! thought Ophelia. *What's going to happen?*

Walter and Father Lou entered the room behind Captain

Ahab, and Lou held up his hands. "It's not what you think! We found Captain Ahab in the church."

"I figured if I was going to meet my Maker, I might as well go where it wouldn't be quite so bad for me," said Captain Ahab.

Do literary characters go to heaven? Linus wondered. Then he decided that was just too much philosophizing for a lad of science.

11:10 A.M.

"Where are you putting Captain Ahab back into the story, Ophelia?" asked Father Lou.

She told him.

"Aye! Perfect!" roared Captain Ahab. And it was a happy roar, if you can quite imagine that. "Here's the plan, Mr. Starbuck. You tell the crew I've come down with some dread disease and"—louder than ever—"KEEP ME IN MY CABIN AT ALL COSTS! I'll write a note saying that you are now in charge of the ship so they can see the order in my own hand."

Starbuck nodded soberly. "What if they don't believe me? And what if you go crazy again, begging your pardon, sir?"

"Oh, I *will* go crazy again! I'm certain of it. You'll have to keep me tied up, my man. If you have to let anybody in on it, it should be Queequeg."

"I agree."

"What did you mean by you having a whale to kill?" asked Walter.

"The great white whale is my own pride, lad." Then Captain Ahab threw his head back and laughed. Personal revelations will do that to a person. What a relief that can be!

The circle began to glow.

"There she blows!" Captain Ahab shouted, giving Ophelia another quick hug and a handshake to the others.

Purple, blue, green, yellow ... the circle pulsed through the light spectrum.

Cato whispered to Ophelia, "I'm going too. They need someone with no respect for authority to keep the captain in his place."

"Bring me a pretty piece of scrimshaw ... Cousin Cato," she said.

The mad scientist opened his mouth to speak, but Captain Ahab's cry prevailed. "The *Pequod* will once again reach Nantucket! Let us onward, Mr. Starbuck."

They stepped inside the circle just as Ophelia leaned down and placed the book on the floor—open to the very spot she'd planned. Just before the white sparks shot up from the floor, Cato Grubs stepped inside as well.

And in a snap, the three men disappeared.

twenty-six

Poor Dears, Another Boring Month to Contemplate—Could I Be Any More Sad for Them?

*T*he trio sat in the park at a picnic table, eating hot dogs from the vendor on the corner.

"That was close," said Linus.

"I don't know if I ever want to do that again." Ophelia took a bite of her hot dog.

"It's hard to believe Cato played the hero," said Walter. "I wouldn't have believed it had I not seen it for myself."

"He's up to something," Linus said.

Ophelia decided she wasn't saying a word.

Linus wished he'd put more chili on his dog. "Look! There's Clarice." He jumped up and hurried over to her. She rewarded him with a wide grin.

"Well," said Walter. "Looks like romance is blooming between two very tall people."

"Yeah …" said Ophelia. She knew it would have to happen someday.

Walter bumped her side with his elbow. "Cheer up. It had to happen someday."

The two finished their lunch in companionable silence.

Ophelia liked that about Walter. In the month between their literary adventures, they'd spent some time together, and it was never forced—always natural and easy.

Walter balled up his piece of wax paper and held out his hand for Ophelia's. He added hers to his and threw them both into the nearby trash can, an easy basket. "There's a new movie playing. Would you like to go?"

"Why not? What's playing?" Ophelia asked.

"A new adaption of *The Three Musketeers*. Have you read it?"

"Not yet. But I'm supposed to read it this summer for English class. I don't know much about Dumas's work."

"Oh, you're going to *love* D'Artagnan. In some ways, he's even loonier than Captain Ahab."

Great, thought Ophelia, *that's just what I need—another crazy. At least this one's fictional.*

Oh. Wait.

So there you have it, readers. Another literary adventure for the trio of Rickshaw Street. I don't know about you, but I wasn't sure Captain Ahab was going to make it back home. Mr. Starbuck and Cato Grubbs have their work cut out for them, I should say!

I'm so happy you've read this second book, but now it's time for me to head back to my closet in the English department and begin working on the next one. I'm sure you can't guess what it's going to be about.

So good night, good day, and good heavens! Go outside! You can't sit around reading all day!

THE END

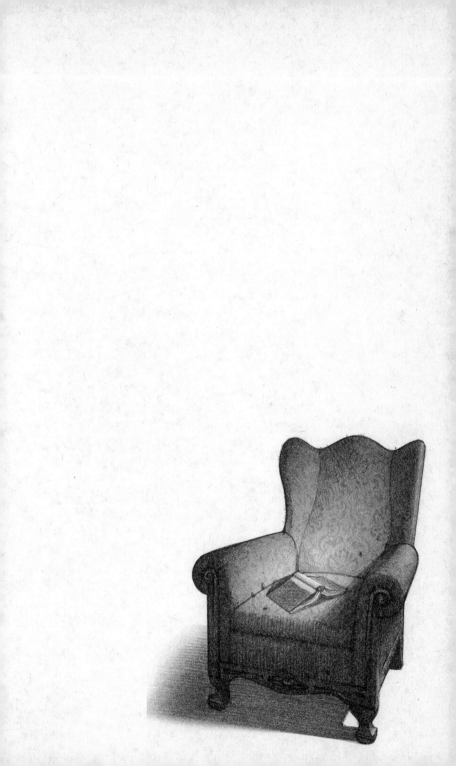

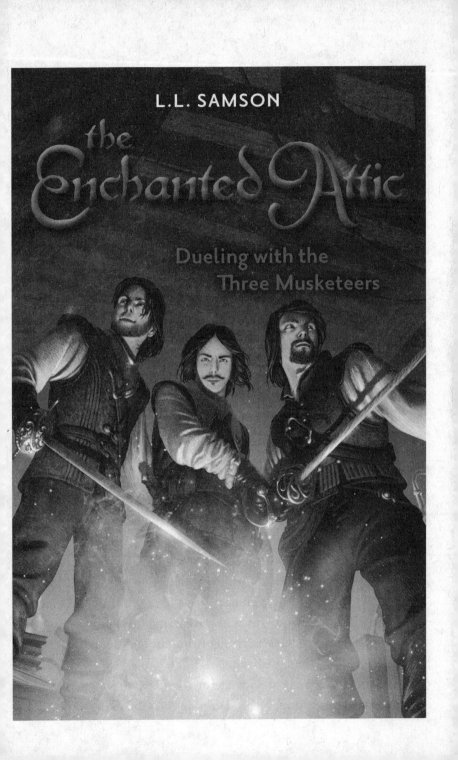

Dueling with the Three Musketeers

one

As if It Wasn't Hot Enough, or, Let's Set Up the Major Conflict Right Away, We'd Hate to Bore You From the Beginning

As twins Linus and Ophelia Easterday slept, the desolate, most middle-of-the-night hour of four a.m. was not the only thing approaching Rickshaw Street and the bookstore where they lived with their aunt and uncle.

As the twins innocently slept, a black-clad figure silently swung open the iron gate of the neighboring building, The Pierce School for Young People, home of Walter, their very good friend and cohort in adventure. The thin, skulking intruder was six-feet-five-inches tall and didn't mind that fact at all. He wore his height without shame, his spine straight and stiff. A messenger bag hung from one shoulder; his steps were measured and precise.

But Linus and Ophelia weren't awake, so when Walter came bursting through the secret door in the bathroom that hid the secret passage between the school and The Seven Hills Rare and Better Bookstore, they didn't hear him either.

He ran into Linus's bedroom and pulled down the sheets on his friend's bed. Linus, six-feet-one-inches tall, sat up automatically. "What?" he cried, raking both sides of his bright blond hair, his blue eyes the size of lemons.

"Hurry, mate!" Walter yelled, pulling his friend out of his bed. "Someone's set fire to the school!"

"Where's Clarice?" Linus asked about his girlfriend as he was being yanked into the hallway.

"She spent the night at her grandmother's house. Come on!"

Ophelia opened the door to her room. "Did I just hear correctly?" She rubbed the corner of her right eye with her index finger. A disgusting glop had settled there, which just goes to show you, even in slumber, no one is completely safe from slimy substances.

"Yes!" cried Walter.

"Did you call 9-1-1?" she asked.

Walter shook his head. "What's that?"

He isn't a dullard. He's just from London.

"9-9-9," said Linus.

Ophelia shot a look at her brother that basically said, *How did you know that and I didn't?* "I'll call. Do not go over there you guys! It's dangerous."

"Right," said Walter.

She hurried down the steps to the kitchen.

"Madge okay?" asked Linus.

Walter assumed a look of horror. "I didn't think—"

"Let's go." Linus hurried toward the bathroom.

Walter followed, they both knelt on the green tile floor and disappeared into the open square next to the bathtub.

By the time the boys emerged in the cleaning closet on the second floor of the school in the boys' dormitory wing, the sirens of fire trucks could be heard coming down the street.

Linus breathed a sigh of relief. If throwing a bucket of water on a little blaze in a trashcan was necessary, well, fine. But he didn't actually relish the thought of becoming a human torch for the sake of a school he couldn't afford, or Madrigal Pierce, (*lovingly* referred to as Madge) the headmistress who constantly snubbed his family.

Walter, however, was on a mission led by his nose. "It's down the stairs. Let's go!" He placed his bottom on the mahogany handrail and slid down in an instant. Linus followed suit. He always liked this place. Imagine a cheerful, clean, haunted house and you might get a clear mental picture of The Pierce School for Young People.

Black smoke snaked out from the back of the house, the private quarters of Madrigal Pierce, the headmistress, owner, fundraiser, math teacher, purchaser, and Jill-of-all trades.

"I didn't realize it was coming from Madge's quarters!" Walter ran through the formal entry hall and back to the hallway leading to the prim woman who made herself the nemesis of everyone she came in contact with. "Breathe deep, mate!"

Linus did.

"Close your eyes!" Walter pushed open the door and smoke hit their faces.

They dropped to their knees and crawled toward Madrigal's bed.

A word of instruction here, dear readers. Listen to the fire marshal when he comes and gives a talk at your school. He has good things to say and you might end up saving a life, someone else's or your own. Whatever you do, don't go back in for your computer. Trust me, a fresh start is never a bad thing and, generally speaking, it's better than death.

The headmistress had already passed out from inhaling the smoke that was billowing in from the bathroom.

They pulled her off the bed. Linus grabbed her wrists, Walter her ankles, and bent double, they slung her from the room and into the main hall. Linus was about to open the door when the firemen kicked their way through.

"At the back!" shouted Walter, then proceeded into a coughing fit.

Men in tan suits with bright yellow reflector striping trampled through with a hose.

Linus, coming out of his coughing fit, leaned down and placed his ear by Madrigal's mouth. "Breathing. Shallow."

"Good."

Not thirty seconds later, two paramedics relieved them of their post at Miss Pierce's side.

As they worked to bring her back to consciousness, one of them looked up. "You might have saved her life."

The boys nodded and watched as the paramedics got Madrigal into a major coughing fit. Neither could bear to see the proud headmistress in such a state. They left the room.

"She'll be okay," said Linus.

Walter couldn't help himself. "I don't know whether to laugh or cry at that."

They sat at the bottom of the grand staircase in the entryway, answering questions, wishing they knew more, watching as a now-conscious Miss Pierce staunchly refused to go to the hospital.

"Let's check on Ophelia," said Linus and they went up the steps.

They crawled through the passage, only to be met in the

bathroom by a rather furious Ophelia, who stamped her foot, her dark curls bouncing in time, and pointed at each boy. "You deserve more than looking like chimney sweeps. I was so worried. I'm furious!"

They both shrugged. After all, a lad's got to do what a lad's got to do.

"Now look at yourself in the mirror and get cleaned up."

She turned and left the room.

"She'll get over it," Linus said. He was used to her bossy ways.

Walter and Linus caught their reflection in the mirror over the sink. Black, sooty faces stared back. Linus's light blue eyes contrasted with his skin like a patch of sky surrounded by storm clouds. Walter's warm brown eyes glowed like amber.

Not that they would have described themselves like that. Heaven's no! Ophelia told me all about it. She visits me in the English Department here at Kingscross University, and, between you and me, she's still mad they went into that house "with no thought for anybody other than themselves." We've all learned not to mention they were trying to save lives. Oh, no! She'll have none of that.

"Good thing Clarice wasn't there," said Walter, turning on the sink faucet.

"Definitely," said Linus.

By the way, Clarice and Linus had become, what they call, "official." What that means to fourteen-year-olds I cannot say, for I haven't an idea, nor do I wish to. Furthermore, I don't think I ever will.

The Enchanted Attic Book One

Facing the Hunchback of Notre Dame

Author: L.L. Samson

A hidden attic. A classic story. A very unexpected twist. Twin bookworms Ophelia and Linus Easterday discover a hidden attic that once belonged to a mad scientist. While relaxing in the attic and enjoying her latest book, *The Hunchback of Notre Dame*, Ophelia dozes off, and within moments finds herself facing a fully alive and completely bewildered Quasimodo. Ophelia and Linus team up with a clever neighbor, a hippy priest, and a college custodian, learning Quasimodo's story while searching for some way to get him back home—if he survives long enough in the Real World.

"A fantasy steeped in classic literature...narrator Bartholomew Inkster brings Lemony Snicket-like irony to frame the story....References to literature throughout the narrative make this a feast for middle-grade book lovers. Kids who like quirky adventure stories with idiosyncratic characters will enjoy a simpler kind of fun."

– Publishers Weekly

Softcover: 978-0-310-72795-8

Available in stores and online!

Talk It Up!

Want free books?
First looks at the best new fiction?
Awesome exclusive merchandise?

We want to hear from you!

Give us your opinions on titles, covers, and stories.
Join the Z Street Team.

Email us at zstreetteam@zondervan.com
to sign up today!

Also—Friend us on Facebook!

www.facebook.com/goodteenreads

- Video Trailers
- Connect with your favorite authors
- Sneak peeks at new releases
- Giveaways
- Fun discussions
- And much more!